A noise rustled nearby in the forest. Keeley jumped up and turned around, dread hardening her stomach.

A man dressed in full hunting gear—his hat low on his face and eyes hidden behind dark glasses—stood behind Brett, holding a rifle.

He'd entered the area in stealth mode, with none of them hearing him.

Strong arms seized her from behind.

Her knees buckled. *Lord, bring help. Now!*

"Bro, we have a pretty one here," the whispered voice said close to her ear.

"Isn't she the one we were told to take?" the other asked.

What?

The man behind her lifted a lock of her hair. "Yup. Redhead. She's the one."

"Who are you, and how do you know me?" Her question could barely be heard over the man's deep breathing behind her.

Brett stood. "Let her go."

A cool blade pressed against her neck as her heartbeat escalated.

She was going to die, and she'd never see her son again.

Darlene L. Turner is an award-winning author who lives with her husband, Jeff, in Ontario, Canada. Her love of suspense began when she read her first Nancy Drew book. She's turned that passion into her writing and believes readers will be captured by her plots, inspired by her strong characters and moved by her inspirational message. Visit Darlene at www.darleneturner.com, where there's suspense beyond borders.

Books by Darlene L. Turner

Love Inspired Suspense

Border Breach
Abducted in Alaska
Lethal Cover-Up
Safe House Exposed
Fatal Forensic Investigation
Explosive Christmas Showdown
Alaskan Avalanche Escape
Mountain Abduction Rescue
Buried Grave Secrets
Yukon Wilderness Evidence

Visit the Author Profile page at LoveInspired.com.

Yukon Wilderness Evidence

DARLENE L. TURNER

LOVE INSPIRED SUSPENSE
INSPIRATIONAL ROMANCE

LOVE INSPIRED® SUSPENSE
INSPIRATIONAL ROMANCE

ISBN-13: 978-1-335-59808-0

Yukon Wilderness Evidence

Recycling programs
for this product may
not exist in your area.

Love Inspired
22 Adelaide St. West, 41st Floor
Toronto, Ontario M5H 4E3, Canada
www.LoveInspired.com

Printed in Lithuania

MIX
Paper | Supporting
responsible forestry
FSC® C021394

To him which led his people through the wilderness:
for his mercy endureth for ever.
—*Psalms* 136:16

In Memory of:

Susan Snodgrass and Caron Tweet
You are missed, my sweet reader friends

Acknowledgments

My Lord and Savior, thank You for walking with us through life's wilderness. Knowing You're right beside us brings comfort.

Jeff, your continual support and encouragement make me smile every day. I think it's time for you to retire and become my full-time PR guy. LOL. I love you.

My agent, Tamela Hancock Murray. You're amazing. Thank you for everything you do for me.

My editor, Tina James. I appreciate you! Thanks for believing in me and my stories.

Darlene's Border Patrol, we've had a rough year and lost friends. Please know how much I love and appreciate all of you. xo

My readers, I'm grateful for your support. Thank you for reading my books.

ONE

Being alone in a creepy forest wasn't how Dr. Keeley Ash expected to start the late-spring day. Normally, she'd be just finishing her botany class at Carimoose Bay Community Campus, but not today. She had called Professor Audrey Todd to take her place. The older woman knew enough about the Yukon's plant life that she could sub in for Keeley at a moment's notice.

It was now almost noon, and Keeley once again squatted in front of a pair of skeletons, studying the plant and tree life pushing through the remains at the base of the aspen in Yukon's Elimac Forest. She'd been tasked to help determine how long they had been buried. Botany was an underutilized form of forensic science in North America, but thankfully she'd proved her skills after she helped solve a case four years ago. The pollen found on the victim's body had also been discovered on a suspect's boot. This, along with other evidence, helped seal the case and convict the killer. Since then, she'd consulted on cases across the Yukon.

Carimoose Bay's forensic department had called Keeley to use her botany specialization to help date the trees growing among the bones. Investigator Cameron Spokene had allowed her to come along to photograph the scene and surrounding areas before they took plant life samples, including a large portion of the tree. They carefully placed all specimens into cardboard boxes, labeling each appropriately. After measuring and pruning the roots surrounding the bones, she took in-depth pictures of the tree and plants to examine when she returned to her lab. Dr. Everson, the anthropologist, had given Keeley permission to investigate the vegetation, as he had to drive from Whitehorse, which was five hours from her present location. He would arrive soon to extract the bones.

She tucked her trowel into her bag and checked her watch. Thirty minutes had passed since she'd last seen or heard from either Cameron or Constable Hopkins—the officer assigned to secure the scene. They had left to load the evidence in their forensics van and also recheck the crime scene perimeter. Neither had returned.

A prickle skittered over her arms, and she shivered. Where were they?

Keeley rose to her feet and unclipped her radio—a necessary tool for the backcountry—from her belt. She pressed the button. "Cameron, need your help at the scene."

Silence answered.

She tried again. "Where are you?" She paused. "Constable Hopkins?"

Nothing.

Movement rustled the pine branches to her right.

Angst bristled the hairs at the back of her neck and cemented her muscles. She extracted the trowel, held it in a vise grip as a weapon and waited. However, nothing appeared.

Keeley adjusted her camera around her neck and strapped her bag across her body. She headed in the direction Cameron and Constable Hopkins had taken. The relentless fog won the battle with the sun and continued to blanket the region, obstructing her view through the trees.

She glanced over her shoulder to get her bearings, but the scene she'd left minutes ago disappeared behind the foggy wall. How was that even possible so quickly? Great. Getting lost in the wilderness was all she needed.

Ignoring the trepidation warning her to run, she continued

deeper into the forest. She required the investigator's help before she signed off and released the chain of custody so his forensics unit could transport the evidence to her lab. There, her trainee, Beth Bower, would begin the process of their examination of the plants. Keeley planned on using this case to help the woman develop her botany skills.

A shadow passed among the trees.

Keeley stopped and listened, her heart pounding. What was that? Animal or human? She held her breath and waited, but the forest stilled.

She pressed her radio button once again. "Cameron, where are you?"

Her voice sounded nearby like an echo. How? She turned in the direction her words had traveled.

She spoke again. Seconds later, she heard herself ask the same question.

Cameron was close, but why wasn't he responding? And where was Constable Hopkins?

Keeley crept through the thick bush and moved branches. She ducked under them and stepped into a small grove. She spoke into her radio again, turning toward her slightly delayed voice.

And drew in a ragged breath.

Cameron lay among the trees, multiple stab wounds on his chest and abdomen.

"No!" Keeley raced toward him and dropped to her knees by his side. She placed both her index and middle fingers on his neck, praying for life. *Please, Lord.*

But the forensic investigator was gone.

A moan filtered through the bush to her right.

She hopped to her feet and glimpsed uniformed legs. "Constable Hopkins!" Keeley rushed to his side and checked his vitals. Weak pulse. Also stab wounds.

He required medical attention—and fast.

She lifted the constable's radio and pressed the button, grasping for words to get paramedics here quickly. "Dispatch, Dr. Keeley Ash requesting medical assistance approximately half a kilometer northeast of the reported remains in the Elimac Forest." She noted the puncture wound in the constable's stomach and pressed her free hand on the injury. She had to slow down the blood loss. "Knife wound in Constable Hopkins's abdominal area."

She waited.

"Dr. Ash, where's Spokene?" Dispatch asked.

Keeley sighed. "I'm afraid he didn't make it. Multiple stab wounds."

"Sending paramedics. Are you safe, Dr. Ash?"

Was she? She checked all directions of the grove. Nothing. "I think so."

"Dr. Ash, this is Constable Layke Jackson. I'm en route from Beaver Creek to your location." His deep voice and a siren thundered through the radio. "Do you have any type of weapon to defend yourself?"

She checked Constable Hopkins's duty belt, but his gun was missing. Not that she wanted to think of discharging a gun. She had taken both self-defense and weaponry classes but prayed she'd never have to use the skills she'd learned. "No," she whispered.

"Stay secluded," Constable Jackson said. "I'm about ten minutes out. Paramedics will be there soon, too."

"Understood." Keeley breathed in deep and exhaled. Great. Alone in the woods with a killer and no weapon. Not a good combination.

God will keep you safe. He's got you. She prayed that was true.

She studied the scene as she kept a heavy hand on the constable's wound. Keeley noted a trail of trampled brush leading to where Cameron's body lay. Multiple footprints surrounded him. More traveled to where she now knelt. Some of those were her own, and she regretted contaminating the scene, but

she had to get to the men quickly. She'd forgotten all protocol. *Stupid, Keeley.*

An idea formed. She could take pictures of the scene while
she waited. With her right hand, she lifted the camera hang-
ing around her neck and shot numerous photos, turning the
lens in different directions while keeping her left hand on the
constable's wound. After help arrived, she'd take samples of
the flowers and other plant life. Maybe pollen or seeds had
been embedded in the suspect's shoes. This could link them
to the scene.

After she took photos for ten minutes, movement sounded
behind her. She startled and turned.

Two paramedics and a police constable holding his gun
darted to her side.

"What's the situation?"

Keeley's jaw dropped as recognition dawned on her. She
stared up at the male paramedic, a man she hadn't seen in
five years.

The father to her child.

"Mickey?"

His eyes widened.

The female paramedic stepped forward. "Brett, who's
Mickey?"

"Mickey was the nickname my buddies called me back
in college." Brett knelt. "Keeley Ash? Wow. It's been years.
How are you?"

Keeley swallowed to contain her emotions and gestured toward the fallen officer. "Been better. He's bleeding heavily."

Brett nodded and inched closer, grabbing gauze. "Okay,
remove your hand."

She obeyed.

He pressed the gauze on the wound. "Tina, we need to sta-
bilize him and get him to the hospital." The pair attended to
the constable.

Keeley had so many questions for Mickey—Brett—but they'd have to wait. She turned to the constable. "Are we safe?"

He holstered his weapon. "I'm Constable Layke Jackson. I checked the area and didn't see any suspects. Can you tell me what happened?"

"I was examining the scene north of here, gathering samples. Cameron and Constable Hopkins went to load the evidence into the forensics van. When they didn't return after thirty minutes, I came looking for them. Found this scene." She shot to her feet. "I need to take plant samples."

"I've read about the cases you've helped with throughout the Yukon. Your botany experience is valuable."

"I wish everyone felt the same as you, Constable Jackson." She peeled off her bloody gloves and removed her bag to grab another pair. "Unfortunately, people forget there's valuable evidence hidden in the plants at a crime scene." She put on her gloves.

"What are you going to do now?"

"Take samples of the plants around Cameron and Constable Hopkins." She gestured toward the forensic investigator. "They also may have pollen under their nails or on their bodies."

Constable Jackson addressed the paramedics. "You both okay? I just want to do another sweep of the area."

They nodded.

Keeley moved carefully to Cameron's body. Her gut told her the suspects still lingered nearby, and she wouldn't let this valuable evidence be destroyed if they returned. She had to act fast. For now, she'd ignore the father to her son, who had just stumbled back into her life. The question was—how long would he stay?

Keeley went into her botany zone and did what she did best—examining the plant life and collecting samples. She inserted them into a small cardboard box from her bag.

Ten minutes later, a noise rustled nearby in the forest. She jumped up and turned around, dread hardening her stomach.

A man dressed in full hunting gear—his hat low on his face and eyes hidden behind dark glasses—stood behind the paramedic, holding a rifle.

He'd entered the area in stealth mode, with none of them hearing him.

Strong arms seized her from behind.

Her knees buckled. *Lord, bring help. Now!*

"Bro, we have a purdy one here," the whispered voice said close to her ear.

His foul breath told Keeley he'd already been drinking.

She recoiled from the rotten combined smell of cigarette smoke and whiskey.

"Isn't she the one we were told to take?" the other asked.
What?

The man behind her lifted a lock of her hair. "Yup. Redhead. She's the one."

Lord, help me!

"Who are you, and how do you know me?" Her question could barely be heard over the man's deep breathing behind her.

Brett stood. "Let her go."

A cool blade pressed against her neck as her heartbeat escalated.

She was going to die, and she'd never see her son again.

Paramedic Brett Ryerson's pulse pounded in his head, not only from the dangerous situation in the forest but also from the woman being held at knifepoint. A woman he let slip through his fingers. "Keels, stay still. I'm here."

A twisted, confused expression flashed over the redhead's face, and Brett remembered. He'd given her the nickname on their first date. He had met the beautiful Keeley at a party in Whitehorse. Brett had just finished his courses when he'd trained to be a police officer. They had dated for a few weeks, and their powerful connection hit him hard, but once he graduated, a constable position he couldn't refuse became available in Ontario. Plus, he wouldn't do a long-distance relationship. He'd seen what it had done to his parents when his mother lived abroad with Doctors in Foreign Lands for months at a time. His parents' marriage suffered from it.

Shortly after moving to Ontario, everything fell apart for Brett. During the first couple of months, he learned quickly that policing wasn't his calling because of his mistake that cost his partner's life. Since he had also studied in the medical field, he resigned to become a paramedic. Thankfully, he had taken the proper science courses in high school and college, so the career fit nicely with his plans to switch occupations. It was the best decision he'd ever made, but the reason he left the force still haunted him today.

A similar situation to what lay in front of him right now. A hostage at knifepoint. Would it end in more deaths, like years ago?

Determination squared his shoulders. Not if he could help it.

Brett took a step forward. "Let Keeley go."

"Is this a reunion?" The hunter with the straggly shoulder-length hair pressed the knife harder into Keeley's neck. A thin line of blood trickled from where the tip punctured her skin.

A tear rolled down her cheek as fear contorted her face.

"Please, you're hurting her. Take me instead." Brett lifted his hands in surrender.

"How touching." The other hunter raised his shotgun. "Well, we have an interesting situation on our hands here."

"What do we do? We were only told to bring her." Long Hair adjusted the bandanna across his face. Dark glasses hid his eyes.

"Shut up, little bro. Let me think." The bearded man tapped his chin.

The constable groaned and shifted his position, bringing Brett back to the situation.

He eyed the wounded constable. Where had Jackson gone to? Ugh! It was up to Brett to save Keeley and the others from whatever plan these two hunters had cooked up.

He raised his hands and gestured toward the bleeding constable. "Listen, this officer needs medical assistance. You have one death on your hands. Do you want to add more? How about you let us all go so we can help him? We won't pursue you. I promise."

Tina moved forward.

Brett hauled her back. "Stay behind me," he whispered. His former police training resurfaced as takedown scenarios ran through his mind.

But no successful ideas formed without someone either getting stabbed or shot. *God, if You're there like Dad says You are, show me what to do.* A month ago, Brett had returned to his hometown after getting a panicked call from his aunt, stating his father's cancer had progressed, and he required full-time care. Brett had immediately put in for a transfer, hoping a position opened up. He hated to leave Ontario so quickly, but his father came first.

The hunter kicked at a stick in his path. "You think we're dumb?"

Brett noted a figure lurking in the trees out of the suspects' sights. Constable Jackson had returned. Brett had met this officer on a recent call. Layke Jackson's wife was a border patrol officer at Beaver Creek and was pregnant after doctors told her she probably would never birth a child. *God protect us. This man is about to become a father.*

Jackson pointed his index finger toward Keeley.

What was he trying to say? Save Keeley?

Brett concentrated on her. How could he overpower the man with the knife and keep both women safe? He must try. He turned back to Jackson and nodded.

First, he had to distract the men. "I never implied you were dumb. Far from it."

The man sneered, revealing a silver-capped tooth. "You got that right, bucko."

"Why did you hurt these men?" Brett shifted his gaze back to Jackson, moving slightly to get closer to Keeley, but not enough to catch the hunter's attention.

Jackson raised three fingers.

In three.

Once again, Brett dipped his head in acknowledgment. He looked back at Keeley and captured her attention. He inched his elbow in an upright position and thrust it backward, hoping she'd catch his drift.

Her eyes widened, but he caught her slight head tilt.

"I ain't telling you anything." The hunter shifted his rifle. Brett turned his attention back to the hunter and Jackson. He raised two fingers.

Brett fisted his hands at his sides and prayed Tina wouldn't react to what he was about to do. He took another baby step toward Keeley.

Two.

Lord, give both Jackson and me strength to overpower this duo of hunters.

Another step.

One.

"Now!" Jackson advanced through the trees, pointing his gun. "Police! Let her go!"

"Tina, down!" Brett barreled toward the other man.

Keeley screamed and elbowed her captor in the stomach.

He grunted and shifted backward but kept his grip on the knife. "Why, you little—"

Brett slammed into the suspect, cutting off the man's words. The pair stumbled to the side, but not before the blade sliced into Keeley's arm.

She cried and clutched the wound.

A shot rang out.

Brett regained his footing from the scrummage and pivoted to face the other hunter.

The man thrust his rifle's butt into Jackson. The constable slumped.

"Nice try." The man bounded forward and hit Keeley in the head, rendering her unconscious.

"No!" Brett stepped toward Keeley.

"Stay back." The older suspect aimed the shotgun directly at Brett. "We don't want you."

"Why do you want Keeley?" He noted the slightly hidden cardboard box sitting close to the deceased man. Had Keeley uncovered some evidence these men wanted to keep hidden?

"That's our secret. None of your concern."

Sirens sounded in the distance. Other constables had arrived.

"Bro, carry the woman. We're leaving. Now!" He directed the gun toward Tina and addressed Brett. "Don't try anything else, Mr. Paramedic, or we'll shoot your partner. You want her death on your shoulders?" He paused. "Don't think the approaching cops will get far. We're not the only ones in the forest."

There were more hunters?

The man lifted Keeley over his shoulder as blood dripped from her forearm.

Brett's attempt to save her life had failed.

And now he risked losing track of her…again.

"Go, bro. I've got this." The older man planted his stance, pointing the shotgun at Tina. "Don't follow us."

Tina whimpered beside Brett, revealing her frantic state.

Brett raised his hands in surrender. He couldn't risk his partner's life.

Gunfire erupted in the distance.

"See, told ya we weren't alone." The man sneered before he backed out of the grove and dashed after the younger hunter carrying Keeley.

Assured they were gone, Brett turned to Tina. "You okay?"

She bit her lip and shook her head.

Brett clutched her shoulders, getting into her personal space. "Listen, I know you're scared, but we have to tend to these officers. Can you do that?"

She inhaled and exhaled. "Yes."

He gestured toward the fallen constables. "Let's check them, and then I need to go."

"What are you going to do?"

"I'm going after Keeley. I can't leave her alone with those men."

Tina scrunched up her face. "The boss won't like that. You're new here, remember?"

"I'll explain everything to him. Keeley is hurt and needs my help."

Brett spoke into his radio. "Paramedic Ryerson requesting additional officers and an ambulance at my known location. Be aware of armed hunters."

The radio crackled. "Officer Len Antoine here. We're en route. Encountered resistance, but two shooters took off. Other officers are in pursuit. Heading your way."

Jackson mumbled and opened his eyes. His hand flew to his head.

"Ryerson, I've deployed another ambulance," Dispatch said.

Brett turned to Jackson. "Let's get you stabilized."

After that, Brett would find Keeley.

Not only did she need medical attention but help staying alive from the dangerous hunters who commandeered the Elimac Forest.

TWO

Water splashed onto Keeley's face, jarring her awake. Pain seared her arm as she attempted to identify her surroundings.

"Wake up, princess," a sinister voice whispered in her ear.

His foul breath brought the memories of the attack back into focus.

She wiped away the water and cowered from his closeness. "Get away from me!" She rubbed her throbbing forehead. A goose egg had formed from the abductor's previous assault. Keeley jumped upright, but the room spun and she plopped back down. Her fingers grazed a crudely applied bandage around her arm where the blade had penetrated. Why treat her wound when they were probably going to kill her anyway?

The earlier events plagued her with questions.

Mickey! Was he okay? And why did the other paramedic call him Brett? She'd met Mickey at a party and they'd instantly bonded. Keeley had dated other men throughout her university years but never fallen for someone after one dinner. Their connection grew after their brief relationship, but then out of the blue, Mickey broke it off, stating the police force in Ontario had offered him a position. He wouldn't do a long-distance relationship.

"Best break off whatever we have now before we both get hurt," Mickey had said. "Besides, I have lots of baggage."

She realized then she'd fallen for him harder than he had

for her. She'd brushed off the sting and threw herself back into finishing her doctorate in botany.

A month after he left, she discovered she was pregnant. She tried to find a Mickey Ryerson in Ontario but failed. Checked all social media platforms. Nothing. Now she understood why. Mickey wasn't his real name. Why lie? Five years had gone by without MJ knowing his father. Their brief relationship had all happened before God tugged at her heartstrings and transformed her life. Even though she realized her mistakes, one blessing emerged.

Michael Joshua—MJ—was the love of her life and brought her joy. Being a single parent had been challenging, but with her mother's help, Keeley finished her schooling and got her doctorate in botany. Ironically, Keeley and her mother, Chief Justice Olivia Ash, always had a shaky relationship. Keeley never knew her father. He died from a heart attack when she was one. God had failed to save her father and robbed her of knowing him, so she rejected God.

When she gave birth to MJ and gazed into her child's eyes, she no longer doubted God's existence. She decided at that moment to go back to church, surrendering her life to Him. She'd hated that she couldn't find MJ's father, but she raised him as a single mother.

And now, Mickey—Brett—had reappeared. It had shocked her to see him earlier, and she was even more stunned to realize he'd become a paramedic. He'd left to join the police force in Ontario.

What was his story?

"Princess, are you in there somewhere?" The man adjusted the bandanna wrapped on his chin before pushing the dark glasses farther up his nose. He had fastened his shoulder-length hair into a ponytail.

His look reminded Keeley of a character from an old Western movie. Who exactly were these men?

He shook her shoulders before slapping her face. "Get with it. We need ya to concentrate."

She winced, and her hand flew to her cheek, the sting burning. "What do you want from me?"

"The evidence you took back there by them bones."

She flinched. What did this hunter know about these victims? Did he have something to do with their deaths? *Play innocent and get more information.*

"What are you talking about? What bones?" The team had loaded the evidence from the skeleton remains into the forensics van, and she'd signed the chain of custody over to the investigators to transport. *Please, Lord, help them to have made it to Beth at the lab.*

Keeley had left the other cardboard box of the latest samples by Cameron's body. She clenched her fists as remorse over the investigator's senseless death threatened to bring tears. *Stay focused. There's time for mourning later.*

As the man carried Keeley over his shoulders, the jostling had woken her briefly, and she had removed the camera, dropping it next to a group of pine trees. She didn't want to lose the valuable pictures she'd taken, and her gut was telling her they were important. Turned out, her instincts were correct. She'd obviously uncovered something these men wanted to remain hidden.

"Our leader sent us to nab you and get what yous collected."

"Your leader? You mean the other hunter?"

He chuckled. "*Pfft.* Naw. He just thinks he is."

Definitely a rivalry going on between the two. She could use that to her advantage. Play them against each other. "Exactly who are you guys?"

"I ain't sayin' nothin' more." He walked to a table and took a swig of soda.

She scanned her surroundings. The hunters had taken her to a run-down cabin somewhere deep in the forest. At least,

that was her guess. Multiple antlers lined one wall, while tro-
phies were displayed proudly on top of the fireplace mantel.

A chill scampered down her body as a thought emerged.
"I'm freezing. Can you start a fire? Please." She exaggerated
rubbing her arms. Perhaps the smoke would lead someone to
their location.

At least, she prayed that would be the case.

"Fine." Her captor lifted matches from the mantel and lit
one, throwing it into the premade tepee of logs. The fire ig-
nited, and soon the scent of smoke permeated the small cabin.

Keeley glanced at the window to determine the time of day,
but the attached cardboard blocked the outdoors. Heat rose
and flushed her cheeks as panic silenced every muscle in her
body, immobilizing her. *Lord, please help someone find me,
and help Brett be okay.*

"Come on. Tell me where it is." The younger hunter withdrew his knife and traced the tip along her chin. "Or I will
mess up your purdy face."

She raised her hands. "Did you find anything on me? I
don't have it."

"You was playing in the flowers, Miss Boto-nist."

Her jaw dropped. "How do you know so much about me?"

"We's got our ways."

"Who's 'we's'?" She must keep him talking to determine
anything to use against them, or to help identify them if she
ever escaped her captivity. "Where's your partner?"

"Ya think I'm stupid, don't ya?" He stood and walked to
the hearth, poking at the logs. "I might not have graduated
from high school, but I ain't dumb."

"I never said you were. Tell me your name." Something
told her this guy was the weaker link between the two. She
peeked at the door. Could she make a run for it? Perhaps distract him first? *Think, Keeley.* She had to get back to her son.
The thought of leaving him alone in this world, if something
ever happened to her, broke her heart.

And now…she had the strong desire to tell MJ she'd found his daddy.

"I ain't sayin' squat." He paced the room.

Wait—the other hunter had called him *bro*. "Are you and the other guy brothers?"

The man turned. "Maybe."

So they were.

"Is it just the two of you?"

The door burst open, and the older hunter appeared, shotgun in hand. "Don't tell her anything. She won't like it."

She?

"I didn't." The younger brother raised his hand. "I promise."

"Did you find out where she hid it?"

"Nope."

"Do I have to do everything?" He approached his brother and cuffed him on the side of the head.

The older brother definitely was the leader—and more dangerous.

Keeley slowly rose to her feet. "Listen, I know nothing and won't say anything. Please, just let me go."

Voices mumbled from a machine on a nearby desk.

The older brother raised his hand. "Shhh…listen." He turned up the volume.

"Suspects last seen heading north from the scene. Rising smoke spotted in the distance. Pursuing on foot. Paramedics are transporting victims to the hospital."

The older brother snatched his water bottle and sprayed it on the flames. They sizzled from the sudden action. "How could you be so stupid, little bro? Now we need to leave."

"She said she was cold."

"So, your soft spot for a purdy lady won out again, huh? Just like that hiker."

Keeley stiffened. She remembered something in the news about missing hikers from a year ago. The case had grown cold. Could that be who these brothers referred to? They killed them, and it was the hikers' bones the police discovered?

"Approaching the cabin now," a voice said over the scanner.

"Bro, grab your gun. We're gonna have to fight our way out." The older brother pulled a walkie-talkie from his cargo pants pocket. "I and D need assistance at the huntin' cabin. Stat."

There were more of these brothers? A shudder snaked down Keeley's spine.

"Roger dodger, bro," another voice said.

"How far out are ya?"

"Ten minutes. Were settin' traps for those coppers. Then we'll—"

"We know you're in there," a voice boomed from outside. "Come out with your hands on your heads."

"Keeley!" Brett shouted.

She jumped to her feet. "Mickey! Help!"

"Shut your trap." The older brother backhanded her hard across the face.

Keeley fell onto the couch.

The hunter ripped the cardboard from the window and stuck his shotgun through a hole in the bottom right of the glass, firing a shot. "We's got a hostage. Stay back or we kill the lovely Dr. Keeley Ash."

How did this band of brothers know so much about her?

Lord, save me. Keep Mickey—Brett safe so I can tell him about his son.

Brett leaned against a tree, studying the small cabin hidden deep in the Elimac Forest. After he had mentioned his former police training and need to treat Keeley's wound, Constable Jackson agreed to let Brett tag along since the other constables were farther out. Brett's leader threatened to fire him when he explained he was helping to rescue Keeley. He argued paramedics didn't engage in confrontation—that was the constable's job. However, Brett couldn't wait. Keeley's life was at stake.

As Brett waited for Jackson to update him on the other constables' progress into the woods, visions of Brett's first shoot-out that had ended his policing career flashed through his mind. Similar to today's events, suspects had taken a hostage at knifepoint—Brett's partner. They had stabbed her before shooting the witness they'd been protecting. Brett had tried to save both, but failed. He didn't have the tools at the scene to bring her back to life. That catalyst had thrust him into becoming a paramedic.

He wanted to save lives and never feel helpless again.

But now a different woman lay beyond the cabin's walls at their mercy. Could he and Constable Jackson save Keeley?

She had stolen his heart over six years ago—too quickly for his liking. They'd bonded fast in their short dating stint. Would he get a second chance with the beautiful redhead to explore the idea?

Or would God take that from him, too?

First, his mother had been killed, and now his father was on his deathbed. The cancer had progressed quickly, and the doctors had suggested to Brett yesterday he get Harold Ryerson's affairs in order. He probably had less than three weeks to live.

And the possibility of losing his father crushed his heart. His dad was his best friend. When Brett lived in Ontario, they'd spent hours over video chat talking about their favorite hockey players. Just last week they'd watched a Rangers versus Leafs game.

How could his dad have deteriorated so fast?

Jackson darted to a tree closer to Brett. "I realize you have a former police background, but we need to wait for backup before breaching the premises. Constable Antoine is close."

"Something tells me Keeley doesn't have that long. These hunters are reckless and dangerous. I saw that firsthand."

"Agreed. They've already killed our forensic investigator and injured Hopkins." Worry crinkled the man's brow.

"He's in excellent hands. We stabilized him before my partner and the other paramedics transported him to the hospital."

"Thank the good Lord."

Constable Jackson's radio squawked.

"Say again, Antoine."

"I'm approaching from your rear. The other constables aren't far behind."

"Copy that."

Brett's muscles locked as alarm traveled through his body. *Hurry!* Keeley needed him.

Seconds later, Constable Antoine emerged from the tree line and approached. "What's the play?"

Jackson studied the cabin before speaking. "Okay, I'm gonna circle around to the rear and see if there's a back entrance."

"Let me do that," Antoine said. "You stay here and cover the front in case the other constables come."

Brett gestured toward the building. "I'm coming, too. I need to tend to Keeley's wound. I'll wave to you if I find a door."

Jackson puffed out a breath. "I don't like you being so close to the danger, so stay behind Antoine. He's armed. You're not. I'll distract them by trying to get their attention. Brett, if Keeley is able, get her far away from the cabin and tend to her wound. We'll cover you."

"The others are close." Antoine motioned toward the side of the cabin. "Let's go!"

Brett and Antoine scooted behind another aspen tree to the right. Slowly, they crouch-walked as they made their way to the cabin's rear.

Brett followed standard police procedures. Funny how they came back to him when necessary. Muscle memory or God?

His father would say God, but Brett had a hard time believing that. God wasn't listening to Brett's pleas to heal his dad, so why would He listen now?

Brett suppressed thoughts of God and skulked from tree to tree, following Antoine and making his way through the woods. Finding a perfect position for spying, they peered around the tree trunk and observed the cabin's rear. The two windows at the back were obstructed, but he noted a door. Perfect.

He shifted to a spot where he had a line of vision to Constable Jackson, then waved.

The constable cupped his hands around his mouth to act as a bullhorn. "We just want to talk. Tell us what you want in exchange for Dr. Ash."

"We's don't negotiate," a voice yelled.

"Please. No one else needs to die today."

Brett veered to the side of the cabin after Antoine, keeping himself low. With their backs against the log wall, they inched closer, one on each side of the door.

Antoine peeked inside the small door's window, then motioned for Brett to do the same.

Brett complied. The dusty glass obstructed his view, and he carefully wiped to clear a corner before looking through.

Keeley sat on a couch facing him. Across the room, one hunter leaned into the window with his shotgun raised. The other stood beside Keeley, his hand resting on her shoulder.

Fury coursed through Brett at the thought of this man touching her. His former attraction to the woman returned, and he pried his gaze away, resting the back of his head against the cabin. He breathed in and out, trying to slow his heart rate. *Stay calm, Brett.* If he was going to help Keeley escape, he had to keep his emotions in check.

He let out a slow, elongated breath and once again looked through the glass.

This time, she spotted him.

Her eyes widened.

He raised his index finger to his lips, indicating for her to keep silent.

She dipped her head slightly, her eyes averting to the hunter standing with the shotgun by the window.

"Give it up, man. You're surrounded." Constable Jackson's voice rose a notch.

An indication of deception. Brett knew the signs and also realized the constables still hadn't arrived. Jackson was attempting to buy time.

It was up to the three of them to save Keeley.

Brett raised his index finger again to show her to wait for a second.

Once again, she tipped her head, acknowledging his instructions.

"You get ready to breach. I'll signal Jackson." Brett returned to the side of the cabin, caught Constable Jackson's attention, then raised five fingers before switching his grip to appear as a fake gun.

Five seconds.

Then shoot.

Jackson nodded and hurried to another tree closer to the cabin, positioning himself to enter.

Brett returned to his spot opposite Antoine. "I'll motion to Keeley we're breaching in five seconds. You ready?"

Antoine lifted his nine millimeter and nodded.

Brett once again stared into the cabin.

Keeley's eyes remained on him.

He elevated his five fingers and then made a pushing motion to instruct her to nudge into the man beside her.

She nodded.

He slowly counted to five, depressing each finger one at a time.

On one, he waited for Jackson.

A shot echoed through the forest.

Antoine thrust open the door. "Police! Hold it there!"

Brett inched into the cabin at the same time Keeley plowed into the man beside her.

The hunter at the window turned at Brett and Antoine's appearance, pointing at them. "Bro, get these guys. I'm busy. There are more coppers here."

The man beside Keeley raised his gun toward Antoine, his finger twitching on the trigger.

Antoine fired.

The young man dropped his weapon and clutched his opposite hand, yelling in pain.

The other hunter turned. "Little bro!"

It was enough of a distraction for them to act and Antoine motioned toward the door. "Get Keeley out of here."

Brett nudged her forward. "Keeley, run to the trees!"

She bolted through the rear exit.

He followed, glancing over his shoulder to ensure they weren't being pursued.

Shouts from out front revealed other constables had arrived to help. Thankfully. They would protect Jackson and Antoine. Brett had to get away from the cabin as fast as he could and protect the woman in front of him.

Was that possible with a band of hunters on their tail?

THREE

Pain burned Keeley's arm as blood seeped through the bandage. Wrenching free from the younger brother's hold had reopened the knife wound. Adrenaline pumped through her veins, giving her strength to run despite the throbbing in her arm and head. However, would the rush of energy be enough to outrun these brothers while more lurked somewhere in the forest?

Gunfire erupted behind them, and she prayed for safety. *Lord, thank You for bringing Brett to me, and keep the constables alive. Stop these men.*

The sudden appearance of Brett shocked her but filled her with relief. He'd risked his life to come after her. Something she wouldn't forget easily.

More gunfire sounded, interrupting her thoughts. She skidded to a stop. "We need to help the constables."

Brett halted. "Backup arrived just as we escaped the cabin. Constable Jackson told me to get you to safety." He gestured her forward. "We need to distance ourselves. Then I want to look at your arm. You okay to keep going?"

She nodded.

So much she wanted to say.

So much she wanted to ask.

But for now, she'd press on.

Fifteen minutes later, Keeley stumbled on a root, but she clutched a branch to prevent her fall. Her legs wouldn't allow her to proceed. "Need. To. Stop." Her breathless words came out like a child whining after a few hours of travel. However, her previous adrenaline had waned, zapping her strength. She leaned against the tree, inhaling and exhaling.

Brett pointed. "Let's take a break and hide behind those bushes. We're too out in the open here. I'll help you."

He wrapped his arm around her waist, and together they trudged into the secluded bushes.

Keeley looked left, then right. "Where are we? I have a terrible sense of direction."

"We're north of the cabin. These woods have grown since I was a kid, so I have no idea."

Keeley nestled between branches, sitting on the ground. "Why did the other paramedic call you Brett?"

"Let me see your arm first, and then I'll explain."

She held out her bloodied, bandaged arm.

He gingerly unwrapped it and pushed on the wound.

She winced.

"Sorry, just trying to get a better look. It's not deep but requires stitches. Looks like the bleeding has stopped. For now." He brought out gauze from his pocket and placed it on top before adding a bandage. "This will have to do until we can get to a hospital. I only stuffed a few things in my pockets before I followed the constable to rescue you. The others were otherwise engaged, and I needed to help find you to treat your injury."

"Tell me your real name."

His gaze snapped to hers. "Brett Michael Ryerson."

Her eyes locked with his, and her heartbeat ratcheted up a notch at his nearness. She remembered how she'd fallen for his baby blues.

Keeley couldn't fall again. Not for her sake—or MJ's. The last man she thought she loved had left them both broken-hearted and confused. She promised herself she wouldn't put MJ through the pain of loss. MJ had taken to Preston fast, just like Keeley.

She wrenched her arm away, averting her stare to the ground. "Tell me why you lied and said your name was Mickey."

He changed his position and leaned his back against a log. "Not entirely a lie. I was young and foolish back then, Keeley." He harrumphed. "Even though it was only six years ago. My college buddies started calling me Mickey instead of Brett. They said it would go over with the girls, so we all made up nicknames for each other. It stuck until I moved to Ontario."

She observed the man before her. How could he have grown even more handsome? Now wasn't the time to ponder their past relationship. *Focus, Keeley.*

He rubbed the bridge of his nose. "I'm sorry I never told you my given name. Like I said, I was foolish and let peer pressure govern my actions back then. I've grown up in the past six years."

A shadow passed over his face before he fixed his attention to peeling the bark off the log.

Something had happened to him, and she desperately wanted to uncover his story. Did it have to do with why he switched vocations? *Keeley, not now.* "When did you move back to the Yukon?"

"A month ago." He let out a ragged sigh. "My dad has cancer. I came back to help take care of him. He doesn't have long."

"I'm so sorry." She read the sorrow in his saddened eyes.

"Why are you here? Didn't you live farther north?"

"Yes, but my mother was offered a prestigious position—Chief Justice Olivia Ash."

Brett whistled. "Wow, the Supreme Court. Impressive."

"Yup, and she found a job for me teaching botany at a campus here in the area. So, I moved my…"

Could she tell him about his son now? Here when they were on the run? She fingered her collar and remembered something from earlier. She popped to her feet.

She had to retrieve her camera before the brothers did.

Brett rose. "What is it?"

She gripped his arm. "We have to go back. When the brothers were carrying me, I woke for a minute and removed my camera. Something told me to hide it, so I dropped it near pine trees close to the cabin."

"You want to go back into the line of fire? You can find the camera later."

"You don't understand. The younger brother let something slip that makes me believe he knew we had uncovered bones. He kept asking me about the evidence I had and said, 'She's the one,' like they knew exactly who I was and what I did." She brushed weeds from her pants.

"How is that possible?"

A question she'd been asking herself ever since her conversation with the duo. "No idea. He also mentioned hikers."

"Hikers?"

"A man and woman vanished over a year ago, but the case went cold after all the clues to their whereabouts had diminished. I'm guessing these brothers know exactly who those bones belong to, and they wanted to stop me from proving it."

"Wait—these hunters are brothers?"

"They kept calling each other *bro*, and the younger one didn't deny it when I asked." She dug her nails into his arm as the urgency of the situation plagued her. "Plus, there are at least two others, and he also referred to a woman. Not sure in what capacity. If the police can catch the younger one, we can use him against the others. He feels like the weak link. We have to go back." She lifted her sleeve and checked her smartwatch. Midafternoon. She also had to pick up her son—his son.

He peeled her fingers away and unhooked his radio. "Let me see if I can get in touch with anyone. Check out the situation first. I don't want us to walk back into a raging fire—so to speak."

She squeezed his shoulder. "Wait—switch your channel. The brothers had a scanner and are listening."

Brett obeyed.

After discovering the brothers had escaped, Constable Jackson assured Brett through the radio that the hunters had fled. They created a diversion, and when the constables stormed the premises, they were gone. An area sweep had proved useless. It was like the hunters had disappeared.

Somehow Keeley doubted that. These brothers appeared to own the forest. They were somewhere close. Her gut was screaming at her to stay away from the creepy cabin.

But the evidence on her camera warranted their return to the lion's den.

Brett positioned himself in front of Keeley twenty minutes later, as they approached the grove near the cabin. The one place he didn't want to revisit, but the one place Keeley had to return to. "Get behind that tree. I want to study the area before we rush back there."

Keeley tugged a band off her wrist and fastened her red hair into a ponytail as she situated herself behind the aspen. "Still have some cop left in you?"

"Always."

"Why did you become a paramedic?"

"Later." But would there be a later? Would they go their separate ways once they retrieved the camera and he safely escorted her out of the forest? For all he knew, she was married or had a boyfriend.

He checked her wedding ring finger. It was bare.

That still meant nothing.

And why did he care suddenly? It wasn't like he'd been thinking about dating again.

He restrained the exhalation wanting to escape. Her presence today had refueled the electricity between them he remembered from six years ago. How was that possible?

His buddies Zac and Mitchell had labeled him a player when they first met. Zac had even challenged his dating life and lack of commitment. The jolt made Brett change his casual ways. His actions would horrify his Christian father, and that, too, drove him to become a better man. Sure, he still dated, but after a woman claimed he'd fathered her child when he hadn't and another betrayed him, his faith in women faltered.

So, why even think about a *later* with Keeley when his trust factor was at the bottom of the barrel? *You know why.*

He shifted his position and ignored her penetrating stare. Her hazel eyes had always been his undoing. *Stop.*

Time to focus on the scene before him. He analyzed every hiding spot in the area, but thankfully, the forest was silent.

All except for the constables scouring the cabin's perimeter. Brett radioed to Constable Jackson, confirming their approach.

The man gave them the green light.

Brett tucked the radio back on his belt. "Okay, let's go. Where did you drop the camera?"

The duo emerged from their hiding spots and advanced toward the cabin. Multiple constables surrounded the area, on guard for further threats.

"Well, I was in and out of consciousness, but I remember seeing a group of pines before the cabin. That's when I unsnapped the strap and gently threw it. I coughed to cover up the sound and then slumped, pretending to be unconscious. After a surge of pain, I really passed out again and didn't wake until the younger brother threw water on my face." Keeley circled the small area, checking the trees, then stopped. "Over there."

She dashed toward a cluster of pines that reminded Brett of a Christmas tree lot. He'd loved searching for the perfect tree with his father as a boy.

Keeley squatted in front of the shorter pine, reaching between the branches. She pulled out a camera held by a strap and a cell phone attached. "Got it!" She unhooked the phone and swiped the screen, then grimaced.

"What is it?"

"My mother's numerous texts from earlier. Seems like she's wanting to get in touch with me."

"Still trying to run your life?" Brett remembered Keeley complaining of her judge mother's ruling thumb. It had extended from the courtroom into her daughter's life.

She scrolled, then froze. "No."

"What?"

"Something's wrong. I need to call my mother." She clicked on her phone. "No service. Great. Not sure what she wanted. Time to get out of here. I also need to ensure all the evidence made it to my lab." Keeley stuffed the phone into her pocket.

"Let's check in with the constables quickly before we leave." Brett strode over to Constable Jackson. "Any updates on the other constable? Did the paramedics make it out of the forest okay?"

"They did. Constable Hopkins is still in critical condition." Jackson addressed Keeley. "You okay?"

"Tired but fine. Did Forensics send the evidence to the lab?"

"Yes. Your employee, Beth Bower, signed for it all." He pointed at the cabin. "Tell me about the men who took you."

Keeley recounted everything she had told Brett. "Did you find anything in the cabin to uncover their identities?"

"Nothing yet, but constables reported two assailants at the entrance earlier, so that makes four. This sounds like the Diglo brothers to me."

"The who?" Brett asked.

"A notorious gang suspected of many crimes in the area, but nothing we've been able to prove." Jackson fished out his notebook and flipped through his pages. "Here it is. Reports of a couple of armed robberies and assaults. No one has ascertained their names or any witnesses. Seems everyone fears these brothers and isn't talking."

"I can see why. The older one is especially scary and dominates the younger. I believe they have something to do with the skeletons found earlier today. Maybe the evidence links them, and you can finally convict them."

"Yes, and solve the missing hiker cold case. The female

was the mayor's daughter. He was not happy when we told him we had no leads."

"Hopefully, the coroner can identify the victims after Dr. Everson finishes with the bones. Is there anything else you need from me? I have to make a call and get to my lab."

"First, Keeley, I'm taking you to the hospital." Brett held out his hand to the constable. "Good to see you again."

"You too." Jackson shook both of their hands. "Thanks for your help. Stay safe. I'll get an officer to escort you."

A constable bounded from the cabin waving an item. "Jackson, look—"

Movement rustled in the trees to their right.

"Fire in the hole!" a voice shouted seconds before a rocket launched from the tree line.

"Get down!" Jackson commanded, unleashing his gun.

Brett knocked Keeley to the ground, covering her body. His pulse spiraled out of control.

The rocket-propelled grenade blasted toward the cabin and exploded into a fireball, the boom deafening anyone in the area. Debris sailed in all directions.

Brett lifted his head just as a chunk of wood whacked Jackson's arm. The constable's weapon flew out of his hand, landing beside Brett.

Gunfire erupted from his left. The younger brother stood with his weapon aimed at Keeley, his intent clear.

Brett scrambled upward and snatched the nine millimeter at his feet, firing multiple shots.

The younger hunter dropped.

"No!" the other brother screamed before glaring at Brett. He pointed at him. "You're a dead man!" He retreated into the forest.

Brett waited for further shots but none came. A question arose. Where were the other two brothers?

"Constables, secure the area," Jackson hollered as he moved

to a crouched position and spoke into his radio for emergency services.

Brett handed Jackson his weapon. "Sorry, my instinct took over when I saw the shooter."

"Good shot. That happened so fast. I'm going after the rocket launcher. Brett, check to see if the suspect and constables need medical attention. These brothers won't get away with attacking our own. Not on my watch." His angry tone revealed his elevated emotions. He sprinted after the suspect.

"Constable, you okay?" Keeley yelled as she rose to her feet.

"Stay low." Brett observed the cabin.

The blaze would quickly spread if firefighters didn't get there fast.

Constable Antoine sat up. "I'm good."

Keeley hurried over to the younger brother.

"Wait!" Brett ran after her. "He could still be dangerous."

Keeley knelt beside the man and lifted the bandanna from his face. She sucked in a breath. "I've seen him before."

"Where?"

She paused as if searching her memory. "I don't remember."

Brett placed his fingers on the man's neck. "He's gone." He searched his pockets for some type of identification but only found a picture.

He gazed at it intently. A young redheaded boy wearing a backpack, leaving a school with a woman. He handed the photo to Keeley. "Do you know this boy?"

She looked at the picture and blasted upright. "No!"

He pushed himself to his feet, grazing her arm. "Keels, who is it?"

Her eyes widened before softening. "My—your son."

What?

He had a son?

And now the boy was in danger.

FOUR

Keeley caught Brett's contorted expression as he raked his fingers through his short dirty-blond hair and stepped to a cluster of trees, obviously distancing himself from her presence. What was the emotion overtaking him?

Confusion? Doubt?

You don't believe me. Not that she blamed him. It was a lot to take in after just reuniting with an old flame. Perhaps that was all she had been. For her, it was more. She had fallen deeply for him. Maybe even loved him. Was that possible after only a few dates? Many of her friends had believed in love at first sight. Not her mother. Chief Justice Olivia Ash's analytical mind could never comprehend something so rash. So illogical.

However, Keeley's broken heart had disagreed with her mother's thinking. She *had* strong feelings for MJ's father.

Keeley strode to where he stood and placed her hand on his shoulder. "Mick—Brett, it's true. MJ is your son, and right now, he's in danger from these men. We have to get back and contact my mom."

He turned, his expression shifted to one of contempt. "How can I believe you?" His words held both sarcasm and anger.

She stumbled backward, away from the sudden rush of disdain permeating from him. "I wouldn't lie about something like this."

"No? Other women would."

What did that mean? She fisted her hands, curbing the anger from overflowing. "Well, I'm not other women. Trust me. MJ is yours, Brett. You can take a DNA test if you want."

"Maybe I will."

Keeley studied his handsome face. Another emotion replaced his previously caring expression, and she didn't like it. Perhaps he wasn't the man she'd thought. She positioned the camera case strap across her body. "Well, obviously something has happened to you over the past few years, because this isn't the Mickey I knew. Then again, you lied to me about your name. Maybe you've never been truthful to me about anything during our short dating time. I need to—"

Constable Jackson jogged to their sides. "You guys okay?"

"Fine." Keeley pursed her lips as she glanced at Brett. "Any signs of the other brother?"

"None. It's like he vanished. I'm guessing the hunters are familiar with these parts of Elimac Forest and know where to hide. I've called in firefighters. They should be here anytime." The constable squeezed Brett's shoulder. "You okay? You're ghastly white."

Brett shifted his gaze to hers, then back to the constable. "I'll be fine. Listen, I need to check on the other constables and then get Keeley back in town. She needs stitches. We okay to leave?"

Jackson turned to Keeley. "We have to take your statement on today's events."

Keeley had to get to her mother's and check on MJ. She didn't have time for statements. "I have to attend to a family emergency. Can I come to your station later?"

"Of course."

Twenty minutes after Brett ensured the other constables on the scene were okay, Keeley followed him through the forest and back to her vehicle. The fog had finally cleared, but the woods still held an eerie silence within its grip.

Or could that perhaps be the tension between them?

Keeley reached into her camera bag and dug out her key fob. "I can take you back to your paramedic station."

"Keels, you need stitches." His softened expression replaced his earlier hardened one.

"No, I need to get to my mother's home. I'll go to the hospital later. Our—*my* son needs me. Don't you need to get back to work?" Not that she expected Brett to take the news of his son lightly, but his reaction had upset her. She never gave him any deceitful signs. She'd always been that proverbial open book.

Maybe that was her downfall. Too trusting. Her track record had proved it, and her son had paid the price. She remembered his tortured little face when she had told him Preston wouldn't be coming around any longer. He'd been heartbroken, perhaps more than Keeley.

She wouldn't let another man hurt her son again. Perhaps introducing MJ to his father wasn't such a great idea.

However, she refused to withhold from her son the opportunity of knowing his father. But would Brett leave again?

"I'm sorry for my earlier reaction. Let's just say…I have trust issues with women."

There was a story behind his words. "I never lied to you before. Why would I start now?"

He hung his head. "I know. It's not you. It's me."

Clearly. Keeley hit the button to open her SUV. "Where do you want me to drop you off?"

He lifted his gaze to hers, studying her. "I'm coming with you."

"Thought you didn't believe me." She opened her door and climbed into the driver's seat.

He jumped in beside her. "I'm not saying I do, but I have to know. If MJ is my son, I will not let him down."

"Understood. I need to call my mom." Keeley hit the Bluetooth and speed-dialed Olivia Ash.

"'Bout time you called. I've been frantic. Didn't you get my messages?"

Keeley gritted her teeth. She didn't need her mother's attitude right now. "Mom, I will explain everything when I get to your place. Let me talk to MJ. Now." She started the engine, then drove out of the park's entrance and onto the highway, which would take her back into town.

"I can't. They. Took. Him." Her mother's broken words came in between sobs.

Terror seized Keeley at her mother's erratic state. Her hand flew to her chest, willing her sudden rapid heart palpitations to slow. "What? Who?" The picture in her coat pocket of her son at the school told her the answer to her question.

Somehow the Diglo brothers had gotten to MJ. A haunting question arose.

Why had they targeted Keeley and MJ?

Lord, please don't take my son. Please.

Brett squeezed her shoulder. "We need to call the police."

"No! Don't know who they are, but they said no police, or they'd kill MJ. Who's with you, Keeley?"

How could Keeley explain what had transpired in such a short period of time when she herself didn't truly comprehend everything? "I'll tell you when I get there, Mom. See you in ten minutes." She punched off the call and accelerated, gripping the steering wheel like it was a lifeline to a drowning victim. *Lord, that's how I'm feeling. In over my head. Help me get above these deadly waters.*

Brett withdrew his cell phone. "I'm going to touch base with my supervisor on the way. He'll be wanting an update." He tapped the screen. "And I need to tell him I'm taking a personal day." He dialed his supervisor and explained the situation.

Ten minutes later, Keeley yanked open her mother's front oak door and scurried inside the five-bedroom luxurious estate. "Mom, where are you?"

"Living room." Her mother's weakened voice stopped Keeley in her tracks. The normally stoic woman had been reduced to tears. Keeley couldn't remember a time when she'd seen her mother cry. Nothing fazed the woman.

Keeley bounded into the room and fell in front of her mother, sitting in her favorite rocker. "Where's MJ?"

Fresh tears tumbled down Olivia Ash's forlorn face as she raised her cell phone with a shaky hand. "They have him."

Keeley viewed a picture of her gagged son with a caption below it:

Tell your daughter to stay out of the forest or her beloved son dies. Chief Justice, pay up or he also dies. No police or he dies. We're watching.

Keeley gasped and burst upright.

She felt Brett's presence behind her. "We'll find him," he whispered.

Her mother sprang out of the rocker. "Who are you? Wait. You!" She charged into his personal space and poked him in the chest. "I recognize your face from a picture my daughter showed me. Where have you been for the past five years?"

Keeley slid in between her mother and Brett, creating elbow room between them. "Mom, let me explain."

Her mother stumbled backward. "If he'd been here, maybe MJ wouldn't have been taken."

"What? Mom, this isn't Brett's fault."

Her glaring eyes shifted toward Brett. "Isn't his name Mickey?"

"Long story, which we don't have time for. Is this the only message you received from the kidnappers?" Brett shoved his hands into his pockets.

"So far, yes." The fifty-five-year-old judge positioned herself in front of the bay window overlooking her enormous front yard.

"Mom, tell me what happened." Keeley's pulse intensified at the thought of her son at the mercy of the deadly brothers. She dropped into a nearby chair and buried her face in her hands. "I can't lose him."

Brett squatted in front of her. "I'm here. I can help."

Keeley lifted her head and examined his face. Could she trust him to stay and help after his previous angered response to the news of his son?

Her mother turned from the window. "How can you help?"

"Mom, don't—"

The house landline rang, the shrill noise echoing through the still room.

Her mother snatched the cordless phone from the coffee table and hit the speaker button. "Olivia Ash here."

"Good. We know you're all together, as we've been watching," the distorted voice said. "You can't hide from us. Let's get down to business, shall we?"

Keeley ran to her mother's side. "Where is my son?" She failed to suppress the anger burning inside.

"Patience, Dr. Ash. Patience."

"What do you want from us?"

"Simple. Judge, we want five hundred thousand dollars wired to our account in the next three hours."

Her mother grimaced. "I can't get that kind of money so quickly."

"Of course you can," the caller said. "You're a judge, after all."

Keeley leaned closer to the phone, attempting to focus in on the voice. Even though they had used some sort of distortion app, the tone and words the caller used were familiar. "Who are you? Do I know you?"

"No more questions. Dr. Ash, you stay out of our forest and you'll see your son again. If not, he dies. Easy peasy."

Keeley's knees buckled, and she stumbled but held on to a nearby chair. "I want proof he's still alive. Now!"

Brett wrapped a protective arm around her waist.

A commotion sailed through the phone. "Mama?"

"MJ! Are you okay?" Keeley leaned into Brett's supportive hold.

"I'm okay. God's with me, Mama. But I'm hungry and just want to come home."

Keeley's heart hitched. "Soon, baby. Soon. I'll—"

"Okay, that's enough. You have your proof. We'll text the ransom instructions. You have three hours. Remember, no police." The resounding click followed by a dial tone blasted into the spacious living room.

Keeley dropped onto the couch and sobbed, unable to hold her emotions in check any longer. MJ was her entire world.

Would she see her precious son again?

Brett hesitated, not knowing how to respond to Keeley's breakdown. He looked at her mother—the Honorable Chief Justice Olivia Ash. She, too, seemed cemented in place. Wouldn't a mother know how to console her only daughter? Had their relationship deteriorated even more since Brett and Keeley dated?

After another sob, Brett couldn't take it any longer and rushed to Keeley's side, bringing her into an embrace. "Shhh. We'll get MJ back. I promise."

Keeley recoiled from his hug and popped to her feet. "How can you say that? You don't even believe he's yours." She walked to the window.

"Why would my daughter lie?" Olivia's harsh tone revealed her anger.

Brett struggled to suppress his temper. "That's a long story, and we don't have time to get into it."

The judge's cell phone dinged, and she swiped the screen. "Instructions from the kidnapper."

Keeley raced back to her mother's side and plopped onto the couch. "What does it say?"

"'Wire five hundred thousand into the account below. Don't try tracing it. Then Keeley must come to the park across from

MJ's kindergarten at exactly six p.m. and sit on the bench on the northeast side. You'll then get instructions on where to find MJ. Any deviation from this plan and he dies.'" Olivia's voice quivered on the last words. "Who are these people?"

"Why the charade of having to go to the park? I don't like it. It puts you in danger, Keels." Brett rubbed his chin stubble.

She shrugged. "Not sure, but I have to follow their instructions to the letter, or I won't see MJ again." She bit her lip.

"Do you think it's the Diglo brothers?" Brett rubbed his tightened neck muscles. "You were with them longer."

Olivia bolted to her feet. "No! Not them. Word in the criminal justice realm says they're extremely dangerous. And smart. They've evaded capture, and no one has been able to identify any of them."

Keeley's jaw dropped. "And Brett killed the younger brother."

"What?" Olivia latched on to her daughter's hand. "Why didn't you say that before?"

"I haven't really had the chance, Mom." Keeley gave her mother the abridged version of their day. "Brett, do you think this is payback for you killing one of them?"

"The timeline doesn't add up. You said your mother had been texting you all day. Olivia, when did you get the picture of MJ?"

The woman checked her phone. "Eleven this morning."

"Our altercation happened after that. Besides, I'm not on their radar. I haven't been back in town that long." Brett wanted to add that they wouldn't know he was MJ's father— if he was indeed. No sense in adding heat to an already blazing situation.

Why can't you believe?

A question his father had asked many times. Harold Ryerson had been referring to God, but in this case, Brett couldn't believe he had a son.

He needed proof.

However, he also wouldn't leave Keeley alone to deal with MJ's abduction.

"Mom, give me your phone. I want to read the instructions again, and you need to make arrangements to get the money." Keeley held out her hand.

Olivia passed it to her. "I'll go call my banker. I have to move some funds around." She left the room.

Keeley removed the elastic from her ponytail and twirled a red lock of hair. Over and over.

A habit he had noticed on their dates. She was nervous.

Brett sat beside her. "What are you thinking?"

She raised the phone. "The sentence structure. It's too perfect. The brothers I met today didn't talk like this. They used 'we's' and other slang. It's not them."

"Could it be the woman they referenced?"

"Perhaps." She tossed the phone on the coffee table and wrung her hands together. "I need my son back."

"We'll get him."

She tilted her head. "Why won't you believe he's yours?"

He stood and paced. "I've made many mistakes in the dating game."

She drew in an audible breath. "You think I was a mistake?"

He turned.

Her widened eyes flashed annoyance.

"I don't mean you, Keels." He returned to the couch and sat, taking her hands in his. "You never lied to me."

"Exactly. So why would I now?"

"Let's just say others have." He hung his head. "I need proof."

"You're a doubting Thomas."

He jerked his head up and stared into her hazel eyes. "A what?"

"You know. Thomas wouldn't believe Jesus was who He'd claimed. He needed to touch Jesus's scars first." She grazed her fingers along his stubble. "MJ is yours, Brett."

A tremor slivered down his spine from her simple gesture. *Don't do this to me.* His gaze traveled to the text message still showing on Olivia's phone.

He jolted upright as he remembered the earlier conversation with the kidnappers.

"Keels, the caller said they're watching us." His alert senses escalated, and he darted to the window, studying the perimeter.

Movement in the bushes caught his attention.

Someone was indeed out there...watching.

Stress thundered in Keeley's head at Brett's proclamation of someone watching. She placed her hand over her heart, willing the storm forming inside to slow. *Lord, protect us. Protect MJ. Calm the waters.* She gathered strength and shuffled to Brett's side. "Do you really think someone is out there?"

"I do. At least, that's what my gut is telling me." He pointed to the bushes by her mother's gate. "I saw movement a second ago. I think we should call Constable Jackson."

She caught hold of his arm. "No! They said no police. Besides, you have training. You can defend us."

An emotion passed over his handsome face before she could label it. Fear? Anger?

He shook his head. "I have no weapon."

Keeley studied the bushes. "I don't see anything. Maybe it was an animal."

"Perhaps."

"Brett, why did you stop being a police officer? You were so excited about it when we dated."

"That's a story—"

Her mother stormed into the room, interrupting their conversation. "Okay, it will take a bit, but everything is in place. How do we know they'll hand MJ over? What if I transfer the money and it's all for nothing?" She sank down on the couch.

Keeley eyed her mother. The woman had become unraveled

at the thought of losing her grandson. Her mother had the same faith, but lately she'd stopped going to church. Why, Keeley didn't know. Her mother wouldn't say when she had asked.

"Mom, it's gonna be okay. We need to trust God." She sat beside her on the couch. "He's in control."

Her mother swatted the escaped tear away with her manicured nail. "Is He? Where was He when they abducted MJ, and why are you so calm? You're his mother!"

Keeley sprang to her feet. "Did I look calm a little while ago? I'm struggling, too, Mom, but I have to trust that God is in the middle of this storm. He's the only thing that's keeping me from falling apart. If I don't have my faith, I don't have anything."

Did she really mean those words? Lately, she'd been wrestling with doubts about God's presence and His direction over her path in life. What was this circumstance telling her? *Lord, show me.* Guilt punched her in the stomach. Why couldn't she have the same faith like MJ? Faith without questions. *Help my unbelief.*

She moved to the window and folded her arms, gazing at the blossoming spring foliage.

Brett cleared his throat.

She turned.

He picked up a poker from the fireplace stand. "A weapon. I'm going to walk the perimeter while we wait. I want to confirm no one is out there."

Her mother rose to her feet. "The gate to the property is secure. No one can get in."

"I just want to be sure. Stay in the house, okay?" Brett left.

Keeley watched from the window as Brett walked around the front yard, looking behind the bushes and other foliage. Then he disappeared around the side of the house. After five minutes of searching, he returned to the living room and gave them the all clear.

Three hours later, after her mother transferred the money

into the kidnappers' bank account, Keeley sat on the allotted bench. Her knee bounced in anticipation, and she checked her watch: 6:05 p.m. Five minutes had passed since the last time she looked. *Is that all?* Where were they?

Brett positioned himself at the other side of the park behind the playground. Waiting and out of sight. She'd text him when she got word of MJ's whereabouts. Her mother waited in the luxury of her home. Their home. Keeley longed to get out from under her mother's wings, but being a single parent made leaving difficult. Perhaps one day. Soon.

A young woman pushed two small boys on the swings. The higher they went, the louder they screamed.

Keeley chuckled despite the angst reinvading her previously calm demeanor. Her pendulum of emotions matched the boys swaying on their swings. Her earlier words to her mother tumbled into her mind. *I'm a hypocrite.* She tightened her fingers around her cell phone as if that would bring a text. She keyed in a message to Brett.

They're late. I don't like it.

She waited.

Only a few minutes. Hang tight.

She replied with a sad-face emoji and viewed the spot where she knew he sat. The top of his head towered over the playground equipment.

Keeley tugged on her jacket and shifted her position. If only they'd gotten reacquainted under more cheerful circumstances. Would they have dated again?

Doubtful. Not with his obvious trust issues.

Plus, she couldn't risk him leaving again, not with MJ's little heart at stake.

A ding announced a text.

You passed. You'll find MJ around the corner in the park's favorite tree. But hurry. Sometimes old tree branches break.

No! She vaulted off the bench and raced toward Brett. "Brett, quick."

He jogged toward her. "Did you hear from them?"

She raised her phone in his direction. "We need to find the tree they're referring to."

His eyes widened before his gaze shifted to each tree in the area. "Which one?"

"I have an idea." She approached the two young boys who had vacated the swings. "Hey, guys, can you tell me what tree is your most favorite in this park?"

The older one pointed toward the edge of the path. "That one. It's huge, and my friends love climbing it."

"Thank you." Keeley dashed toward it with Brett close behind. "MJ! Where are you?"

Silence.

"MJ!"

Mumbles sounded from above.

Keeley reached the tree and looked up.

And gasped.

They had gagged and tied her son to a high, partly broken branch. If Keeley and Brett didn't hurry, the limb would break, and MJ would plummet to his death.

She sucked in a breath.

Crack!

The branch snapped, and MJ slipped.

"No!" Keeley lunged forward, extending her arms to catch her boy.

Lord, save my son!

FIVE

Brett ignored the panic coursing through his veins and made his way up the tree, praying the broken branch would hold long enough for him to reach MJ. *Lord, I know we haven't spoken in a really long time, but please hear my plea. Don't let MJ fall. Give me swiftness. Guide my steps.* Brett reached for the next branch and scaled higher.

"Hurry, Brett! You're almost there."

Keeley's cry from below urged him forward. Gave him strength. Or was his sudden rush of adrenaline from God? Perhaps muscle memory from his younger years? His friends had labeled him king of the jungle since he was always hiding in trees, climbing the highest of any of his buddies, to his mother and father's detriment.

Kind of ironic that his first meeting with his son—if MJ *was* his son—would be in a tree. Brett had done his best thinking at higher altitudes. He'd often sought solitude and refuge in the trees.

The boy whimpered, bringing Brett back to the task at hand.

Saving a five-year-old.

Brett had to reassure him and give him hope. "I'm coming, MJ. Hang on. You've got this." Brett lunged for the next branch and lifted himself higher. *Almost there.*

Within moments, Brett reached MJ and removed his gag. "I'm here, bud."

The boy looked up at him, tears glistening in his crystal blue eyes.

Shock stole Brett's breath as he viewed a mirror image of himself, minus the red hair. Could MJ be his son?

Son or not, Brett had to save him. "Wrap your arms around my neck, okay? Nice and tight."

The boy whimpered as his lip quivered. "Are you a bad guy?"

The branch dropped another inch.

MJ screamed.

"What's happening?" Keeley hollered from below. "Save him, Brett!"

They only had seconds before the branch would break from the boy's weight. Brett was shocked it held this long. He focused on MJ. "No. I'm a friend of your mommy's, and I'm here to get you to safety." Brett would properly introduce himself once they were safely on the ground. "Don't be afraid. I'm used to climbing trees and getting back down."

MJ nodded and hung on to Brett's neck.

Brett untied the rope fastening the boy to the broken branch and pulled him away from its deadly grip. "Okay, now wrap your legs around my waist."

MJ obeyed.

"Got him, Keels."

"Thank you, Brett. Mama's here, baby boy." Keeley's voice trembled.

"I'm not a baby," MJ replied.

Brett chuckled. "Of course you aren't. We'll remind your mother of that later. Here we come, Keels."

Now for the hard part. Getting MJ back down the tree. Brett grabbed the rope and tethered himself to the five-year-old, praying the knot would hold. If they fell, Brett would break MJ's fall. "Keep hugging me. Tight as you can."

MJ squeezed harder.

"Good boy. Okay, we're going to make our way down branch by branch."

A gust of wind swept through the tree, causing the limbs to sway.

No! Not now. Brett held tighter to the boy and the trunk, willing the sudden spring wind to remain at bay.

"I'm scared." MJ sniffed.

Brett breathed in. Out. In. Out. He had to cool his own nerves in order to keep MJ calm. "I know, bud. Your mama is praying for us right now." At least, Brett assumed that to be the case. "We're going to inch back down. Ready?"

MJ nodded.

Brett placed his foot on a lower branch and hugged the tree with his free hand, slowly descending limb by limb until they reached the bottom.

Brett untied MJ and tousled his red hair. "You did good, sport."

"You're a good climber, mister."

"MJ!" Keeley squatted and hugged her son. "I'm so glad you're safe."

"Mama! Too tight."

Brett plucked a leaf from MJ's hair. "Keels, he's a brave boy."

She glanced at Brett, tears welling. "Thank you for saving him." Keeley released MJ and held him out at arm's length. "Did they hurt you?"

MJ shook his head before reaching up and wiping away his mother's tears. "I okay, Mama."

Brett knelt in front of him. "MJ, I'm a paramedic."

The boy scrunched his nose. "A what?"

"I look after people who are hurt. Can I check on you just to be sure?"

"'Kay."

"You tell me if any of this hurts." Brett gently squeezed each of MJ's limbs, but the boy didn't respond. "He seems fine, but we need to get him checked at the hospital. Plus, you still need stitches, remember?"

Keeley rubbed her arm. "I know." She turned back to MJ. "This is Mr. Brett."

MJ held out his hand. "Thank you, Mr. Brett, for saving me."

The boy's simple act and words softened Brett's heart. Brett cupped MJ's little hands into his own. "You're very welcome." He addressed Keeley. "Let's go."

"Mama, wait." MJ fished out a note from his pocket and handed it to Keeley. "The man told me to give you this."

She unfolded the paper.

Brett stiffened and didn't miss Keeley's soft inhalation. "What is it, Keels?"

Brett inched closer and peered over her shoulder at the crudely written message.

Dr. Ash, stop your investigation or we'll get to your sweet red-haired boy. Again.

"No!" Her legs buckled.

Brett caught her before she collapsed.

Anger flushed his face and snaked throughout his body at the thought of someone hurting this child.

His protective nature took over, and he steeled his shoulders.

You'll have to get through me first.

No matter what, Brett would pay with his life to protect this boy.

Keeley clung to Brett and snuggled against his chest, her heartbeat mingling with his rapid pulse. If she let go, she was positive her weary legs would buckle. Questions flooded her mind. Who were these people? How did they know so much about the Ash family?

"Mama?" MJ rubbed the backs of her legs. "Don't cry. I okay."

Keeley tensed in Brett's embrace, then pulled back and wiped her tears before turning to her son. "Mama's just so happy to see you again, slugger." She dropped to her knees and caressed his face.

"Slugger? MJ, do you like the Blue Jays?"

MJ jumped up and down. "Yes, Mr. Brett!"

Nothing like her son's love of baseball to lighten their heavy moods. Keeley pushed herself upright. "Shall we head to the hospital?" She had to remain strong and put up a brave front for her son—*their son*.

Keeley examined the playground. She wanted to tell MJ she'd found his father, but right now she was concerned they were still being watched. Later.

First, she had to ensure Brett would stick around. She refused to tell her son about his father if the man was moving away again.

Two hours later, after getting checked by a doctor and discharged, Keeley closed her son's Bible storybook. MJ had fallen asleep after only one page. Tonight, he wanted to hear all about David and Goliath. He said today he'd faced a giant and won. When Keeley and Brett had inquired about his captors, MJ clammed up, not wanting to talk about it.

Keeley hadn't pressed him, but hopefully tomorrow MJ would give them information that could help shed some light on his captors.

Since Keeley wouldn't call in the police, Brett had begged her mother to let him stay with them for protection. Surprisingly, she agreed.

Keeley kissed her son's forehead and turned off the lamp near his bed, leaving only his superhero night-light to illuminate his room.

She backed out and eased the door shut.

Brett's muffled voice drew her toward the living room. She

scuffled down the hallway and stopped at the entrance, not wanting to intrude on his conversation.

"Dad, remember to do everything the nurse tells you, okay?" A pause. "I'll be back tomorrow. I have some news to share." Another pause. "Night, Dad. Love you very much." Brett shoved his phone into his jeans and sighed.

Keeley wrapped her buffalo-plaid housecoat tighter around her body and entered the room. "Your dad okay?"

He turned, his eyes glistening from unshed tears. "Not really." He plunked down in the nearby rocker and wiped his eyes. "I'm not sure how to say goodbye. My dad is my best friend."

Keeley sat beside him on the sofa, placing her hand on his knee. "I'm so sorry. Do you know how long he has?"

"Doctors are saying only a few weeks. I'm in the medical industry and feel so useless. I can't even help my own father."

She didn't miss the waver in his voice. "It's hard to lose a parent. I never knew my dad. He died when I was one."

"I can't imagine not knowing my father."

Keeley removed her hand and leaned back. "Life without my dad wasn't easy, and my mother struggled raising me."

"Has she always been this stern with you?"

"For the most part, yes." Keeley envisioned the day their relationship took an abrupt turn. She pictured it vividly. "When I was six, my mom yelled at me for stepping into her rose garden. I had been playing with a friend and tried to hide. I ruined one bush, so I decided to find some wildflowers to make it up to her."

"So, you've always liked plants?"

She grinned. "Yes. Anyway, to make a long story short, I went into the woods and got lost. I had wandered too far and couldn't find my way back. I got scared and had my first panic attack."

Brett rose and positioned himself by the stone mantel. "Oh my. How long were you in the forest?"

"Until around nine o'clock that night. It's why I have a fear of getting lost." She puffed out a breath. "I'll never forget the harsh treatment from my mother when they finally found me." She raised her wrist, showing a smartwatch. "Now I'm GPS connected all the time. It also has SOS on it."

Brett picked up a picture.

Her favorite photo of her son—their son—on Santa's knee. MJ had howled, and the photographer snapped the shot at the right moment. "He was three when that was taken."

Brett laughed. "Too funny."

"Trust me, he got over his Santa fear quickly, especially after his grandmother spoiled him with lots of presents."

He placed the picture back. "I was the same way at that age. My mother told me I refused to sit on Santa's knee. She had to bribe me with treats."

"Like father, like son."

"I wish I would've known about MJ." He leaned against the fireplace. "I'm sorry."

Keeley stuffed her phone back into her housecoat pocket and fiddled with the belt. She prayed he wouldn't blame her for not knowing his son for five years. "I honestly tried everything to find you. Even called around different Ontario police departments. No one knew you."

"Not your fault. I should have been honest with you from the beginning." He moved back to the rocking chair. "I was young and stupid, thinking I was this macho police officer." He shook his head. "Boy, was I wrong on that one."

She examined his handsome face as past feelings toward him resurfaced. "Why did you change your vocation?"

"I just realized it wasn't for me." He averted his gaze toward the front window, squeezing his lips into a flat line.

Keeley tensed. He held something back. What haunted his time with the police department? Clearly, he still didn't trust her enough to share.

Time to change the subject. "Brett, do you think the Diglo

brothers are responsible for MJ's kidnapping? Something is telling me it wasn't all for the money."

He turned back to her. "You mean like a ruse to get under your skin?"

"Or get close to our family. Maybe this is all about Mom. She's made some pretty powerful enemies in the criminal justice system."

"Do you think MJ will tell us anything about his abductors tomorrow?"

"I'm hoping so." Keeley fiddled with the belt on her housecoat. "If the Diglo brothers are behind this, they've underestimated the Ash family. We don't quit that easily. I collected valuable plant evidence, and I'm determined to figure out exactly what it's telling me."

"Then you won't mind if I talk to the police department and request protection for all of you."

"I'm good with that." She bit her lip. "My mother, on the other hand, may not be. She's more stubborn than I am and likes her privacy."

"I noticed. However, in this case, that's a good thing." Brett returned to his seat. "I'm surprised you still live with her with your strained relationship."

"Well, I'm saving up to buy a house. It's tough being a single parent."

Brett reached over and placed his hand on hers. "I'm here to help. Are you going to tell MJ about me?"

She yanked her hand back. "That depends. Are you planning on sticking around here in Carimoose Bay?"

He exhaled. "Not sure yet. I'm gonna be honest with you. My supervisor in Ontario left my spot open in case I wanted to return. He even hinted at a promotion, but—"

She shot to her feet. "Until you know, we don't tell MJ. I can't break his heart again."

"Again? What do you mean by that?" He stood and reached for her hand, but she retreated.

"You have your secrets. I have mine. I'm heading to bed. See you in the morning." Keeley hurried from the room. She hated her abrupt change in mood, but when it came to her son, Mama Bear took over.

She would do anything to protect MJ.

Even from his own father.

SIX

The pitter-patter of little feet outside Brett's door woke him, but he didn't mind. The sweet boy's charm was hard to resist, and Brett wanted to get to know him better. Especially if he was his son. What would Keeley tell MJ? He had noted her shift in demeanor when he asked last night. Brett couldn't answer her point-blank question on whether he planned on staying in the Yukon. His former supervisor in Ontario had left it open for him to return once his father passed away and even hinted at a promotion—a position he wanted badly. However, could Brett now leave behind a possible son...for a job? He understood Keeley's hesitation. She was only protecting the boy from getting hurt.

Was MJ really his son? He clenched his fists and pounded the bed. His trust issues plagued his mind and prevented him from fully believing. Even though the resemblance to his son was undeniable, he wondered if he should still get a DNA test to be sure. Keeley would never forgive him if he insisted on it. But the last woman who told him he'd fathered a child had lied. He met Paula at a party back in his wayward days. That night was foggy, as he'd had too much to drink, but he was positive he went home by himself. She'd insisted her son was his, but the test proved she'd lied. After that experience, Brett vowed to stay out of the dating game and clean up his life.

Brett checked the time on his cell phone: 8:00 a.m. He'd

missed the numerous texts from his current supervisor. *Ugh!* Why hadn't his alarm sounded? He punched in Fred Swift's number and waited.

"Where have you been, Ryerson? I've been trying to get in touch with you." The man's angry voice sailed through the phone.

Fred's paramedics often said his rough demeanor reminded them of nails on a chalkboard. Irritating and they wanted to run in the opposite direction. But the man had been fair to Brett in the short time he'd been back in the Yukon.

"Sorry, sir. Yesterday was a tough day after the attack."

"Tina didn't give me all the details. Did they catch those responsible?"

"Not yet. Keeley is still in danger, and now her son has been targeted." Brett got out of bed and pulled a T-shirt from the bag he'd packed quickly. "Sir, I hate to ask this, being so new and everything, but are you okay if I take another day? I need to handle getting them protection."

"Why you? How do you know Dr. Ash?"

Brett cringed. How could he explain without revealing all? "I met her a few years ago, and she was in the wilderness when the attack happened." He held his breathing as he waited for Fred's response.

"Ahh…a Good Samaritan."

Brett silently exhaled. "Something like that."

"Fine, Ryerson. You're walking on thin ice, but I know Chief Justice Ash, and I don't want to get on her bad side." He chuckled. "One more day, then I need you back on shift."

The man hung up before Brett could thank him.

The smell of bacon enticed Brett's stomach into hurrying. He tossed his phone on the bed and dressed as he planned in his head how to approach Constable Jackson for additional protection without putting Keeley and MJ in more danger. Just how close were the Diglo brothers watching?

Several loud knocks interrupted his thoughts. "Mr. Brett. Brekky! It's bacon, eggs and pancakes."

Brett smiled and opened the door. "Morning, MJ. Well, that sounds like a delicious breakfast. Did you make it?"

MJ scrunched up his face. "No. Mommy did." He caught his hand. "Let's go."

Brett let the boy lead him into the Victorian-style dining room furnished with an antique mahogany table, chairs and china cabinet.

Olivia sat at the head of the table, sipping from a mug and reading the paper.

Keeley looked up from her position beside her mother and smiled. Her red curls flowed over her shoulders and sparkled from the sun shining in the bright room. The green blazer she wore took his breath away. He'd always loved the color on her.

Brett fought to suppress his attraction and moved farther into the dining room. "Morning, ladies."

Keeley pointed to the coffeepot sitting on a side serving table. "Hey there. Coffee?"

"Yes. I need an extra kick this morning."

Olivia closed her paper. "You're finally up. Keeley insisted we wait."

"Sorry, I slept in." He lifted a mug and poured. "My alarm didn't go off."

MJ scrambled onto a chair and stole a piece of bacon, stuffing it into his mouth.

Keeley's jaw dropped. "MJ! You know better than that. We have to bless the food first."

"Sorry, Mama," he replied in between chews.

Brett restrained the laughter threatening to surface and sat beside MJ.

"Okay, time for grace." Keeley bowed her head and prayed a blessing over the food.

"Amen!" MJ yelled before grabbing more bacon.

"Michael Joshua, simmer down." Keeley's tone revealed her lighthearted mood.

Michael Joshua. "So that's what *MJ* stands for." Brett smiled inwardly. Had Keeley named him partly after Brett?

"Yup. Joshua was my grandpa. Michael is after my papa." His lip quivered. "I just wish I knew him. Mama doesn't know where he is."

Brett gripped his knife and fork tighter, curbing the sudden rush of emotion from MJ's innocent statement. He observed Keeley.

Her eyes widened.

Olivia cleared her throat. "MJ, can you tell us what happened yesterday? How did the bad people get to you?"

Leave it to the judge to address the proverbial elephant in the room.

"Mom, I wasn't going to ask him until after breakfast." Keeley added scrambled eggs onto her plate.

"Well, we need to know." The woman sipped her coffee.

MJ dropped his fork. The clang echoed in the room, silencing them. "I okay, Mama. The arc name-sess-es snatched me."

"The who?"

"Duh, Mama. The bad guy in superhero movies." MJ twisted up his nose.

Brett covered his mouth to hide his grin. He could tell the boy was serious, and Brett didn't want to make fun of him.

"An archnemesis?" Keeley scooped eggs onto her fork.

"Yeah, that's it."

"Do you mean he wore a mask?" Brett glanced at Keeley and raised a brow.

MJ nodded. "Yeah, they wear masks. Those bad guys."

"How did he get you at school, honey? Where were your teachers?" Olivia added fruit onto her plate.

"I had to go to the bathroom, and my teacher's phone rang. The bad guy poked me, and I fell asleep."

Olivia bolted to her feet. "I'm calling that school. They need to be held accountable."

MJ whimpered.

"Mom, stop. You're scaring him." Keeley turned to MJ. "How did you get up in that tree?"

"They made me climb a ladder, then tied me."

Keeley moved closer to her son and wrapped her arm around his shoulders. "Did they hurt you?"

"No. One played checkers with me after they came back with some food."

"They left you alone?" Fire burned in Brett's gut at the thought of these men abandoning the boy.

"Yes, when I was sleeping."

"How many were there?"

The boy counted on his fingers, then raised four. "And their mama, Mr. Brett."

The woman Keeley had referred to earlier.

Keeley jolted forward, her knife clattering to the floor. "Their mama was there, too?"

"Yup. She was nice."

"Did you see what she looked like, or did she wear a mask, too?" Brett took a bite of his bagel.

"Sunglasses. Scarf. On. Face." MJ mumbled between bites.

Keeley huffed and leaned back in her chair, crossing her arms. "I don't believe this." She shifted toward Brett. "What type of mother would kidnap a child?"

He inched closer and didn't miss her lilac scent. "Do you think she's connected to the Diglo brothers?"

"Possibly."

"I need to report this to the police and get you more protection," he whispered.

"Mama, you told me no whispering. Rude."

Keeley bounced back into her position. "You're right, MJ. I'm sorry. Let's finish our breakfast so we can get you ready for school."

"Yay! I'm gonna play with Liam." He turned to Brett. "He's my bestest friend."

Emotion clogged Brett's throat as he thought of his own best friend—his father.

MJ gobbled down the rest of his food. "Done. Mama, can I be ex-cus-ed?" He staggered over the word.

She smiled. "Yes, you're excused."

MJ hopped up and skipped out of the room.

A buzzer sounded.

Olivia walked to a panel on the wall and pushed some buttons. An image of the front gate displayed on a screen, revealing an SUV at the entrance. "Good. They're here."

"Who?"

"Terry and Vic—the bodyguards I called in to protect my grandson." Her eyes flashed at Keeley. "Since you insist on going into work, even after MJ's life was threatened. He needs someone with him at all times."

Keeley stood quickly, her chair scraping on the hardwood floor. "Mom, I can take care of my son."

"Clearly, you can't." Olivia pushed a button, opening the gate. She brushed by them, her heavy perfume lingering in the room. She turned from the entrance, gesturing at Brett while her gaze remained on Keeley. "Now that he's here, perhaps you can quit your job and raise your son. Stop playing in the weeds." She pivoted and continued down the corridor, her heels clicking on the hardwood floor.

Wow. Chief Justice Olivia Ash's claws had emerged, ready to sink into any prey.

Even her own daughter.

Brett had the sudden urge to strike back, protecting Keeley and MJ.

Keeley's shoulders slumped as she walked into her lab at Carimoose Bay Community Campus, her mother's harsh words continuing to haunt her mind. Keeley realized Olivia Ash only

wanted to protect her grandson, but she didn't have to criti-
cize and deflate Keeley in the process. *Mom, I can't deal with
you right now. God, please calm my spirit. I have a job to do.*
Hearing about the people who'd abducted MJ increased her
determination to examine the evidence. The Diglo brothers
wanted something to remain hidden, but Keeley would find it.

If it was the last thing she did.

She opened the lab door, turning back to Brett. "You didn't
have to come. I'm in a secure building." She subconsciously
rubbed the healing wound the Diglo brother had inflicted as
determination to do her job emerged.

"My supervisor agreed to give me today off, too. Besides,
I'd love to see your lab." He grazed her hand. "I know what
you do is important, even if your mother doesn't agree."

"I can't do anything right in her eyes." Keeley twirled a
curl. "It's especially times like these I wish Dad was still alive.
A father would know how to bring the Honorable Olivia Ash
down a peg or two." She entered her lab. "Speaking of fathers,
how's yours doing?"

"I spoke with the nurse this morning, and he's holding on
for now. She's shocked he hasn't passed. It's like he's waiting
for something." He followed her. "I just wish I knew what it
was."

She studied his profile. How could he be even more handsome than when she'd first met him six years ago? She ignored
the sudden rush of attraction. "Do you have any family members he's waiting to say goodbye to?"

"I only have my aunt, and she's been to see him multiple
times. My mother is deceased, and Dad's brother passed three
years ago."

"Well, maybe—"

"Dr. Ash, you're here." Her coworker shuffled toward them
and embraced Keeley. "I'm so glad you're okay, darlin'. Beth
told me what happened."

The woman in her late fifties rubbed Keeley's back in comfort. She always knew when Keeley required a mother's touch.

Unlike Keeley's own. "Thanks, Audrey. I'm doing okay. MJ is safe with my mother's bodyguards."

The woman released her. "Bodyguards?" She rolled her eyes. "That woman."

"Right?" Even her colleagues had seen the judge's ruling demeanor. "Although, MJ loves having them around. When we dropped him at school, he bragged to all his friends that he's under the protection of superheroes."

Audrey chortled and threw her head back. "That's just like MJ." She clasped Brett's hand in hers. "And who's this handsome gentleman?"

"Brett Ryerson, meet Professor Audrey Todd." Keeley gestured to her other colleague. "Brett, these are my coworkers. This is Audrey, and that's Beth Bower."

He waved. "Nice to meet you both."

Keeley leaned in toward Audrey. "This is Mickey."

Her jaw dropped. "*The* Mickey?"

Keeley nodded.

Audrey looked him up and down, whistling. "You failed to tell me how handsome he was."

"Shucks, you're too kind."

She turned back to Keeley. "I'd keep him." Audrey picked up her briefcase from a nearby chair. "Well, I'm off to teach. Got your classes covered today, as I figured you had lots to get done."

"You're a lifesaver. Both of you. Don't know what I'd do without you ladies." Keeley placed her camera bag and briefcase on a table. "Have a good day, Audrey."

"You too, darlin'." She flicked her hand in dismissal. "Ta-ta." She glided out of the room.

Brett folded his arms. "Well, isn't she just something now?"

"And then some." Beth rolled her eyes.

"She certainly keeps us on our toes. She has a heart as

big as the ocean, though." Keeley withdrew her camera and handed it to her assistant. "Beth, can you load these into our system? I want to review them up on the screen."

"Sure can." She gestured toward tables on the other side of the room. "The evidence is all set up and waiting for you."

The middle-aged Beth Bower added another blessing in Keeley's work and personal life. She'd recently been widowed and wanted to try something new, so she went back to school to take botany. She now trained with Keeley, and the two made a great team.

"You're the best. Thank you." Keeley took her lab coat off a wall hook. "Brett, you don't have to stay. Go see your father. He needs you."

"I will soon." Brett's cell phone chimed, and he fished it from his pocket. "Constable Jackson is asking when you're coming to their station to give them your statement."

"Shoot. I forgot about that. Tell him later this afternoon. I have to start examining this evidence. Stat."

"Understood. I'm calling him because I want to get some officers watching your campus and MJ's kindergarten."

Beth sucked in a breath. "You don't think we're safe here?"

"I'm sure you're fine, but I'm not risking it. What can I say? You can't take the policeman out of me." He tapped on his phone and placed it against his ear. "Not after what happened yesterday." He positioned himself by a window that faced Carimoose Bay's favorite turquoise lake as he spoke on his phone.

Keeley's office was on that side of the building and where she did her best thinking. There was just something about staring at the gorgeous glistening water that sparked her mind and creativity. *Thank You, God, for Your creation.*

Speaking of thinking…

Time to work.

Keeley spent the next several hours examining the evidence she had collected and doing a thorough analysis on plant taxonomy. She identified each type of vegetation, pollen and seeds. Spring was in full bloom in the Yukon, and the forest sprang with new life.

At Keeley's insistence, Brett had left to visit his father. She couldn't work with someone hovering, and although she appreciated Brett's concern for her safety, she had to practically kick him out of her lab. He contacted the campus's security team and asked them to watch Keeley's lab closely. They promised to report any suspicious activity to the police. Brett would return later in the day to take her to the police station after he'd made arrangements with Constable Jackson.

She analyzed the tree samples she'd taken of the roots growing from the skeletal remains. She also examined the photographs she'd taken, magnifying each for a detailed look to determine how much the roots had grown.

Her tummy growled, reminding her she'd skipped lunch. Beth had often reprimanded her for getting so immersed in her work that she failed to take care of herself. However, right now, her concern was to study the seasonal rings on the tree and roots. She guided her magnifying glass closer to the vegetation and gasped.

"What is it?"

"I want your opinion, Beth. Come and look at this. These are the thick roots that had grown into the remains. Plus, a section of the tree." She handed the magnifying glass to Beth. "What do you see?"

Beth viewed Keeley's findings. "The light-colored rings suggest growth in the spring and summer. The dark ones later in the year."

"What does that tell us?" Keeley tested her student.

"The remains had probably only been buried close to the tree twelve to eighteen months ago."

"Very good." Keeley flipped to another photo. "Check these plants. What do they tell us?"

Beth inched closer to the screen. "They haven't been there for long."

"Correct. Often when someone buries a body, they disturb the plant life, and other vegetation sprouts up." She pointed. "Now, it is spring, so plants have been dormant for the winter, but study this cluster. Even though they haven't fully blossomed yet, they're taller. That tells us they weren't disturbed." She traced her index finger in a circular motion. "This is the area we need to concentrate our efforts on. I want you to study each sample closely, okay?"

Beth stumbled backward. "Me? Are you sure?"

Keeley clutched onto both of her arms. "Yes. You've got this."

"What are you going to do?"

Keeley checked her watch. "Order us some lunch. Then I'm going to examine the plant life I collected near Cameron's body." She bit her lip. "That reminds me... I need to find out from Constable Jackson who I contact in their forensic department to consult with and share my findings."

"I'm sorry about Cameron. He was such a nice man."

Keeley gripped the sides of the table. "His death was senseless. I need to finish with the evidence and help bring those responsible to justice." Her screen flickered several times. "What's going on?"

Beth wiggled the mouse. "Don't tell me the system is on the fritz again."

The monitor flashed, then went dark.

Keeley froze, her stomach knotting. What—

An explosion rocked the building, imploding her lab's windows. Glass, plaster and other debris hurled toward the pair.

Keeley shoved Beth and dived behind a counter with a thought pummeling through her mind.

She was getting too close.

SEVEN

Brett tucked the blanket closer to his father's neck, checking his pulse at the same time. Weak. Tears threatened to torpedo Brett if he didn't hold his emotions intact. His best friend didn't have much longer in this world. At least hospice had provided a caring nursing staff to attend to Harold Ryerson in his own home. The nurse assigned to him today stood in the corner getting meds ready.

"Don't look at me like that." His father's whisper could barely be heard over the beeping heart machine. "I'm not gone yet, but my Savior is waiting. It will be soon." He drew in a ragged breath.

The nurse darted to the bedside and increased the morphine drip. "That should help with the pain, Mr. Ryerson." She returned to counting meds.

Brett cupped his father's hands in his own, pondering how to word his next question. *Spit it out and don't hold back.* A saying Brett's father often repeated to him when he determined something was on his son's mind. "Dad, what are you waiting for? I'm here. Yes, it's hard to say goodbye, but I don't like seeing you suffer."

His father's gaze shifted to the nurse. "Nancy, can you leave for a few moments? I need to talk to my son alone."

Nancy dipped her chin in acknowledgment and silently left the room, closing the door.

Only the annoying beeping remained.

Brett hated the silence.

Always had, ever since he was a boy. He had told his dad that white noise was his friend. He either had music playing in the background or the television blaring in the next room. At night, he used a sound machine to lull him to sleep.

"Son, I'm waiting for you."

Brett snapped his attention to his dying father. "Dad, I'm here."

"That's not what I mean. Come back to God. He's waiting." He patted Brett's hand. "It's time to surrender to Him."

Brett stood. "How, Dad? God has taken so much from me. First Gideon and then Mom. How can I surrender to Someone who continually fails me?"

"Gideon's death wasn't your fault. It was mine."

Brett's muscles tightened as anger flushed his face. The day his younger brother, Gideon, died slammed into his mind. The annoying twelve-year-old had been interrupting Brett's time with his friends, and Brett finally had had enough. He yelled at him and then took off with his friends, leaving Gideon home alone. Their father was working, and their mother was away on another of her doctor missions.

The fire consumed their home quickly, and Gideon died in the inferno. The fire department had found evidence of several Molotov cocktails, and the police determined a gang was out to take revenge on their father—Constable Harold Ryerson.

"But, Dad, if I'd been home, I could have saved Gideon." Brett closed his fingers into fists.

"If you had been home, I may have lost two sons. That gang was after me and out for revenge. I was supposed to be off work that day but took another shift."

"But why didn't God stop it? Why didn't God also stop the serial killer who took Mom's life?"

Another wave of pain twisted his father's face.

But Brett guessed it was emotional pain, not physical. Even

though their parents had had a rocky marriage with her being away so much, they had held a deep love. Her death not only sparked Brett's journey into law enforcement but ended his father's career. He retired shortly after the killer was caught.

His father reached for Brett. "I need to tell you something about God."

Brett returned and grasped his best friend's outstretched hand, holding on tightly. "What is it, Dad?"

"Sometimes God allows us to enter the wilderness to shape us. Mold us. Then use us. He is in every detail, even life's rough ones." He inhaled a rattled breath. "Let Him in."

"It's so hard." Brett hung his head and dropped into the chair.

"Son, look at me and come closer."

Brett obeyed.

His father reached for his Bible on the nightstand and passed it to Brett. "Read Exodus. God prepared His people in the wilderness. He will do the same for you. Just trust Him."

Brett took his dad's Bible in his hands and traced his finger along the worn leather. "Thanks, Dad. I'll do that."

"Promise?"

"I promise." It was the least he could do for the man who had raised him. "Dad, I don't know how to say goodbye."

"That's easy, son."

Brett's mouth hung open. "How can you say that?"

His father smiled. "We say, 'Catch you later,' because we'll see each other again one day."

Brett's breath hitched at his father's peaceful expression. His smile reminded Brett of MJ's excitement over his new superhero bodyguards. "Dad, I need to tell you something." He fiddled with the buttons on his shirt, pondering how to tell his father the news of MJ. "I think I have a son."

His father's eyes brightened. "What?"

"His name is MJ—Michael Joshua."

"Why do you only *think* he's your son?"

Once again, Brett stood and paced. "Dad, I've had another woman tell me I fathered a child when I didn't. I just don't know if I can believe Keeley."

"Has she ever lied to you before?"

"No, but I really don't know her that well. We only dated a few times six years ago." Brett eased the drapes open, letting a ray of light into the darkened room.

The symbolism wasn't lost on Brett. Was MJ a ray of light in his pain? He turned back to his father. "But you should see him. He has bright red hair and looks exactly like I did at five."

"I want to meet my grandson. Now, before it's too late."

Another promise to fulfill.

But how could he, with Keeley's overprotective nature holding MJ back?

Brett squared his shoulders. He would convince her to give his father this last dying wish.

"I will, Dad. I promise." Brett returned to his father's side. "You will love him. He's such a good kid."

Harold Ryerson's lips curved upward before his eyelids fluttered.

Brett patted his father's hand. "Rest, Dad. You're tired."

"Remember, God is in the details." The sixty-nine-year-old closed his heavy eyes.

A question plagued Brett. Was his father right? Was God in every detail?

His cell phone buzzed, and Brett fished it from his back pocket, swiping the screen. Constable Jackson.

Explosion at Carimoose Bay Community Campus. Thought you'd want to know.

Brett failed to quash his sharp intake of breath.

Keeley needed him.

Questions about God would have to wait.

* * *

Muffled voices sounded in the distance, bringing Keeley back to consciousness. How long had she been out? Her erratic pulse held her in a dark grip. Warmth trickled down her face. She brought her hand to her pulsating temple. A drop of blood greeted her and raised her panicked state. She inhaled, held her breath, then exhaled slowly. Repeating the process calmed her nerves. She shifted her position and winced. Glass slivers bit into her hand.

Pounding steps and shouts nearby pushed through her foggy brain. Help was approaching.

Or could it be someone wanting to finish the job?

Keeley eased up on her elbows and scanned the room for Beth.

She lay still within inches of Keeley's position.

"Beth!" Keeley ignored the spots flickering in her vision and scrambled toward her coworker. *Lord, please help her be okay.*

Keeley placed two fingers on Beth's neck. Steady. *Thank You, Lord.* She gently shook her friend. "Beth, wake up."

The woman stirred and blinked her eyes open. "What. Happened? Pain. Hurts." She struggled to move.

"Explosion. Where does it hurt?" Keeley ran her hands over Beth's legs.

Beth winced. "There. Hit my knee when you pulled me down."

"Sorry. We had to escape the flying glass. I didn't mean to hurt you in the process." Causing pain for this amazing older woman was the last thing on Keeley's mind. But she had to protect her from harm.

"Dr. Ash!" Constable Jackson pounded on the door. "Are you in there?"

Keeley pushed herself upright and staggered to the entrance, unlocking the door. "I'm glad to see you, Constable Jackson."

He entered the room with other officers and paramedics.

"Call me Layke." He glanced around the room. "Are you both okay?"

"I have minor cuts, but Beth whacked her knee."

"I'll check her over." Tina rushed to Beth's side and squatted.

Keeley followed. "Tina, you were in the forest with Brett yesterday. Sorry we have to keep meeting like this."

"I know, right? Haven't seen you in a few weeks, and now you're on every call." She smiled and opened her medical bag. "Wow, you've been attacked twice in just over twenty-four hours? Someone sure doesn't like you."

The male paramedic approached. "I'm Otto. Let me look at your forehead."

Keeley puffed out a breath and let the man examine her head. "Layke, was anyone else hurt?"

"No, it appears the blast was isolated to the room next to yours. We're examining the scene with local firefighters, but my gut is telling me it was deliberate."

So, once again, Keeley was targeted, and this time Beth was put in the crosshairs. She gritted her teeth. *Lord, these people have to be stopped.*

Layke withdrew a notepad. "Can you tell me what happened?"

Keeley winced from the paramedic's pressure. "We were examining evidence, and our screens began flickering, then went dark. Moments later, the explosion ripped out a wall and shattered the windows."

"Your computers were affected?" Layke asked.

Keeley pushed Otto's hand away. "Yes. I need to check the system. I can't lose valuable evidence I've logged."

Otto scowled. "Wait. I need to examine you."

"I'm fine." She returned to her computer and hit several keys, but nothing appeared on the screen. "No!" She pounded the table. "This can't be happening."

"What is it, Dr. Ash?" Layke moved beside Keeley.

She choked in a breath and placed her hands on the table to steady her shaky muscles. "Our computers were in the room next door. Someone wiped them out."

"Backup servers will protect the evidence."

"Only if I saved everything, Beth." She racked her brain trying to remember if she had. She normally did it like muscle memory, but had that memory failed in her weary and shaken state of mind after everything that had happened with MJ?

MJ! She had to check on her son. *Ugh!* She had left her purse in her office with the phone number for the bodyguards. She fumbled for her cell phone and hit her mother's number. *Come on, Mom. Pick up.*

"Keeley, I'm about to head into the courtroom. Not a good time." Her mother sounded out of breath.

"Mom, check with your bodyguards. I need to know if MJ is safe." Keeley failed to subdue her panicked state.

"Why? What's happened?"

"Bomb here on campus."

"Keeley, I told you not to go to work." Her mother's harsh tone revealed her anger.

Keeley gripped her phone tighter. "Mom, I don't have time for this. Just check with them. Please!"

"Fine. I'll call you right back."

Keeley hit End and stuck her phone into her pocket.

Running footsteps echoed outside their door moments before Brett darted through the entrance and to her side. "Keeley! Are you okay?"

"Fine. Just a scrape."

"No, you're not. You're bleeding." He addressed Otto. "She needs her wound cleaned."

The paramedic threw his hands in the air. "I was trying, but she wouldn't let me finish."

Brett crossed his arms, tilting his head. "Keels, let him help you. Why are you so stubborn?"

"My evidence is at risk, and I have to protect it now." Warmth flushed her cheeks. "I can't let them get away. They need to be brought to justice." She turned to Layke. "I hate to ask this so soon, but who's taking Cameron's place as forensic lead?"

"Virginia Volk. She's on her way."

"No, she's here." A thirtysomething brunette entered the room and approached Keeley, holding out her hand. "Call me Ginger. I'm here to examine the scene next door once firefighters have contained any lingering flames from the blast. I understand you were working with Cameron on yesterday's crime scene?"

The constable lifted his hands to get everyone's attention. "Okay, we need to clear the area before discussing this any further." He addressed Otto and Tina. "Do these ladies need to be transported to the hospital?"

"I'm fine."

Brett moved closer and grazed Keeley's forehead. "Thankfully, it's a tiny cut."

"Beth needs to get her knee x-rayed. It's swollen." Tina addressed Otto. "You finish bandaging Keeley's wound, then we'll take Beth to the hospital."

Fifteen minutes later, the paramedics left with Beth, even though she'd claimed she was okay. But Keeley knew better. She read the pain on her face. Beth had only been trying to put up a brave front.

Like Keeley.

Ginger pointed to Brett. "What about him? He's not law enforcement."

"He saved my life, and I want him here." Something told Keeley she'd need him beside her.

Layke nodded. "Agreed. He also has a police background and could prove helpful."

Keeley's shoulders relaxed. "I haven't finished studying all the evidence, but I came to one conclusion today."

Ginger folded her arms, tilting her head. "Okay, I'm not

sure that plants will reveal anything in this case, but what did you find?"

Great—she didn't acknowledge how botany could help solve cases. Keeley would miss Cameron's cooperative attitude. He knew the value of what she had to offer. "The tree roots growing with the remains reveal they'd been there anywhere between twelve to eighteen months." Pain shot through her temple. She waited for the sensation to pass. "Has Dr. Everson given you any information on the bones?"

Ginger extracted a notebook from her vest pocket and flipped the page. "Two remains. One female. One male."

Just as Keeley had suspected. She addressed Layke. "When did you say those hikers went missing?"

"Thirteen months ago." His jaw dropped. "Could this be them?"

Keeley shrugged. "Possibly. Contact the mayor since one of the missing hikers was his daughter."

"Layke, did you identify the deceased man at the cabin?"

"Not yet. No hits on his fingerprints. Either the man was squeaky-clean before this or someone erased any records we may have had on him."

Ginger closed her notebook. "Is he one of those Diglo brothers?"

"Well, since we don't know exactly who they are, we can't say for sure." Layke's radio crackled. "Go ahead, Constable."

"Building has been cleared," the female said. "No further bombs."

"Copy." Layke turned to Keeley. "Dr. Ash, is there somewhere we can go to take your statement from yesterday? I want Ginger to examine the lab and the computer room, so we need to clear out."

"Please call me Keeley. Yes, there's a lunchroom down the hall. Ginger, please preserve my evidence. I still have work to do." Keeley hated to bark orders, but this woman had already revealed her dislike for forensic botany. Keeley wouldn't let anything happen to her samples.

Ginger's lips pursed. "Even if I don't totally buy into forensic botany, I'm a professional. I wouldn't tamper with evidence."

Rein it in, Keeley. "Of course. Sorry, I'm just a little testy with yesterday's and today's attacks." Her cell phone chimed, and she checked the screen before hitting Answer. "Mom, is MJ okay?"

"He's fine. Stop scaring me like that and quit messing around with this investigation. You're putting your son at risk." The woman hung up.

Keeley viewed the blank screen. "And goodbye to you, too, Mom." She crammed the phone back into her pocket. *Wow, you are crusty today.*

Brett grabbed her hand, tugging her off to one side. "What is it? MJ okay?"

"Yes, but my mother is trying to get me to stop investigating, too. Brett, I can't. I have to help solve this case. We need justice for Cameron and for the other two victims." She stared at the cardboard boxes containing the vegetation and pollen samples she'd collected around the investigator's body. She still had to examine those, and something told her time was running out. Wait—

She scurried back to where Layke and Ginger were talking. "Layke, has the clothing been removed from the assailant's body?"

Ginger stepped forward. "I can answer that. Yes, it's bagged and being examined right now."

Layke's radio squawked.

"Constable Jackson, I have news for you," the female constable said. "Sergeant wanted me to tell you the coroner has reported the suspect's body has gone missing."

A collective gasp filled the room.

Layke pressed his radio button. "What do you mean 'missing'? Someone stole it?"

"Affirmative."

Keeley clenched her jaw. How was that possible? Someone desperately wanted to hide the man's identity.

A thought arose, and she snagged Layke's arm. "I need the suspect's boots. They may have valuable evidence on them."

If they couldn't identify the man, maybe the vegetation would at least link him to the crime scene.

Perhaps giving them something to go on and help finding the other brothers.

Whoever they were.

EIGHT

Brett paced outside his father's bedroom as he waited for Keeley to arrive with MJ. She had agreed to let him visit, but Brett could only introduce Harold as his father—not MJ's grandfather. At least, not until Brett committed to staying in the Yukon. She was adamant about not taking the risk of breaking her son's heart. However, Brett knew his father was on borrowed time and wanted to introduce him to MJ before he passed. He could at least fulfill this promise.

Coming back to God would have to wait for now. Brett wasn't ready to put his complete trust in Him until he had proof God really loved His children.

Constable Jackson had finally taken Keeley's statement and had promised to have the suspect's boots delivered to her lab tomorrow once Ginger had finished her investigation. Thankfully, the damage from the bomb was mostly isolated to the computer room. Keeley had determined that she had backed up the files, and they were safe and sound.

But would the perps keep trying to destroy the evidence?

The bell rang, and Brett opened the door.

"Hey, sport." Brett raised his hand, palm out.

MJ high-fived him.

Brett noted the two bodyguards behind MJ and Keeley. Seemed Olivia wasn't letting her grandson go anywhere without protection. "Hey, everyone. Come on in."

Keeley's half smile told him she wasn't happy about something.

Brett pointed toward the living room. "Guys, you can wait in here while MJ, Keeley and I visit with my dad."

The pair remained silent but didn't move.

"We'll be fine. Please give us some time alone."

They nodded at Keeley and left the foyer.

Brett leaned into Keeley. "You okay?"

She huffed out a breath. "Just frustrated with my mother's attitude. We had a huge argument when I told her MJ was coming to meet your dad."

"She doesn't like me, does she?"

"Right now, she doesn't like anyone. She also said you don't need to stay at her house since she now has superhero bodyguards." Keeley rolled her eyes.

MJ tugged on his mother's hand. "But, Mama, I want Mr. Brett to stay with us. Can he?"

Keeley shrugged. "Okay with me. I will tell your grandmother it was your idea. You good with that, Brett?"

"Of course."

"Yay!" MJ hopped up and down. "Who lives here, Mr. Brett?"

Brett squatted in front of the boy. "Someone very special to me. Wanna meet him?"

"Yes!"

Keeley took her son's hand. "Slugger, we have to be on our best behavior, okay? Be nice and quiet."

"Why?"

"Because the man is very sick."

MJ's bottom lip quivered, tears welling. "Is he gonna be okay?"

Shivers tickled Brett's arms. The boy's eyes were filled with compassion for someone he hadn't even met yet. *You're a sweet boy. I really hope you're my son.* "Only God knows, sport."

What? Where did that come from? Maybe Brett's view of God was changing.

He held out his hand. "Let's go."

MJ released his mother's grip and held tightly to Brett, skipping as they made their way toward his father's room.

"Remember, no running around. Can you do that?"

"Yes, Mama."

Brett eased the door open. "We're here. Safe to enter?" He glanced at Nurse Nancy.

She nodded.

Brett opened the door wider and gestured to MJ. "This way."

The boy gawked around the room, his eyes widening when he noticed the nurse. "Is this a hospital?"

"Kind of." Brett led MJ to his father's bed. "MJ, I would like you to meet Mr. Harold. Dad, this is MJ."

His father lifted a limp hand. "Nancy, raise my bed. I want a good look at Brett's friend."

MJ hesitated.

Keeley nudged her son forward. "Go on, honey. It's okay to say hi."

Brett placed a step stool by the bed. "You can stand on this."

MJ obeyed and held out his hand. "Hello, Mr. Harold. I'm Michael Joshua, but you can call me MJ."

"Nice to meet you, MJ." Brett's dad took the boy's hand, and then his gaze landed on Keeley. "This has to be your mother. You have the same beautiful red hair."

"Yes, sir, and freckles." MJ pointed to the spots on his face. "I hate freckles."

Brett's father chuckled. "Oh, but, son, freckles are a sign of beauty."

MJ scrunched up his nose. "I'm a boy!"

The group laughed.

Keeley stepped forward, holding a book. "I'm Keeley. Nice to meet you."

"You too." His dad pointed to the hardback. "What do you have there?"

Keeley held up a Bible storybook. "MJ wanted us to read you a story. Would you like to hear it?"

"Sure would." He patted the bed. "MJ, crawl up here beside me."

MJ looked at Brett. "Is that okay, Mr. Brett?"

Brett struggled to keep his emotions intact. This polite boy was stealing his heart. "Sure is."

MJ climbed onto the bed and stretched out beside Brett's father. "Ready."

Brett pulled a chair closer to the duo. "Sit here, Keels."

She shook her head, handing Brett the book. "MJ wants you to read it." She patted the back of the chair. "Sit."

Brett hesitated. Could he do this?

"Come on, Mr. Brett. Read. Now." MJ snuggled closer to Harold.

His father wrapped his arm around the boy. "Yes, son. Hurry."

Outnumbered.

Brett sat and opened the book. "Which one?"

"How about Noah?" MJ clapped.

"Okay." Brett flipped the pages until he found the story.

Keeley leaned over his shoulder. "MJ likes it when I put on a different voice for each character."

"Are you kidding?" Brett whispered, trepidation sneaking up on him at the thought of entertaining a child.

"Nope. You've got this." Her eyes glistened as a smile danced on her lips.

And caused Brett's heart to hitch. *Don't do that to me.*

He focused back on the page and read the story of Noah and the ark, inserting different voices and animal sounds.

His father's and MJ's laughter warmed his heart, and Brett wrestled with his rising feelings but concentrated on reading.

The group cheered when Brett finished.

His father yawned.

Brett hated for the evening to end, but his father required rest. "Sport, it's time to go. My dad needs to sleep now."

"Not yet. Mama and I always pray before sleep time." He sat upright and folded his little hands. "Can I do it?"

Brett didn't miss the tears in his father's eyes. "Of course, MJ. Go ahead."

"God, Mr. Harold has to go to sleep now. Can You help him to get better? I like him. Amen." MJ cleared his throat. "Oh wait, and can you tell Mr. Brett to stay? I like him, too. Amen."

Brett focused on Keeley's face.

Her twisted expression revealed her surprise at her son's prayer, too. She composed herself and held out her hand. "Time to go, MJ."

MJ leaned forward and kissed Brett's father's cheek. "Night."

His father reached up and patted his grandson's face. "Please come back and see me soon."

"I will! Bye." He scampered off the bed and waved. "Mama, can we go in Mr. Brett's car?"

"Sure." She turned to Brett. "I'll tell the bodyguards that we're going with you. That okay?"

"Sounds good."

"We'll grab the booster seat. You almost don't need it any longer." She ruffled MJ's hair. "You're a big boy now, right? Tallest in your kindergarten class."

"Yes!" MJ stood on his tippy-toes as if proving it to the group.

"Excellent. Just want to say good-night to Dad. I'll be there in a minute." Brett held the door open, letting the duo go ahead of him.

"Son," his father whispered.

Brett turned. "Yeah, Dad."

Tears tumbled down his father's face. "Stop being a doubting Thomas. You don't need more proof. That *is* your boy. He not only looks and sounds like you when you were his age, but his movements are identical. No doubt in my mind."

His father's soft words bull-rushed into Brett, and he stumbled backward.

Could his father be right?

After all, the decorated police officer was known for his sixth sense in all matters of justice—and the heart.

Keeley ensured MJ was buckled into his seat before jumping into the passenger side. "Ready." She checked her watch. "Good, just enough time to see MJ's favorite television show before bedtime."

MJ raised his hands. "Yippee! Let's go, Mr. Brett."

"Yes, sir." Brett chuckled as he shifted the Jeep into Reverse. "ETA fifteen minutes."

Keeley loved how Brett and MJ were getting along. The interaction soothed her soul, and she was touched at how Harold had reacted to his grandson. She could tell that he already adored him. *At least he seems to believe me.* She drew in a deep breath, catching Brett's woodsy cologne, and rested her head against the seat. Feelings for this man were coming back at full force. Already. She had to rein them in. *He's probably not staying, Keels.* Keels. The nickname he'd given her on their second date. No one else called her that, and she liked it. But now? It brought back too much pain and regret.

Brett turned left out of his father's driveway.

She checked the side mirror and noted the bodyguards' vehicle follow, cutting off another car. The driver honked and shook his fist. Their "superheroes" weren't letting them out of their sight. They knew that if they lost the judge's grandson, they'd never hear the end of it from the Honorable Olivia Ash.

And neither would Keeley.

She recalled their earlier conversation when she explained the theory of the skeletal remains being the mayor's daughter. Her mother had yelled at her for breaking the kidnappers' demand of not getting involved. Keeley had tried to explain her commitment to providing any information that would help reopen the cold case and get justice. However, her mother wouldn't hear of it—said she was putting her grandson's life in danger.

Keeley had suspected something else was behind her mother's objections. Normally, the woman was committed to bringing criminals to justice, so what was really behind her anger? Keeley had asked, but her mother bit her lip before storming out of the room—a habit Keeley had come to recognize over the years as the judge withholding information.

Did her mother have a secret of her own?

A car horn brought Keeley back into the present. A white sedan cut in front of them.

Brett braked to avoid a collision. "Whoa, buddy!"

The sedan sped up, but their wheels caught on the gravel shoulder, edging them toward the embankment. They swerved back and forth before losing control, careening into the ditch on the other side of the road before plowing into a tree.

MJ screamed. "Mama! Accident."

"Oh dear. I gotta stop. They may be hurt." Brett put his four-ways on and pulled over. He hit the Bluetooth button and called 911, requesting emergency services at their location.

A man staggered onto the road, holding his head as blood trickled down his face. He raised his other hand and beckoned them to come.

Brett cut the engine. "Stay here."

The bodyguards parked behind them, and one hopped out, racing toward Keeley's side. He tapped on the glass.

Keeley hit the button to open the window.

"You guys okay?" The bald, muscular man leaned into the car to check out MJ in the back seat.

"We're fine." Keeley unfastened her seat belt. "Brett, I'm coming, too. MJ, go with Terry. Mama has to help."

Terry tilted his head. "Are you sure that's wise?"

"MJ has both of you. We'll be fine. I'm sure I saw two people in that vehicle."

Brett clasped his door handle. "I agree with your superhero on this one, Keels."

She scrunched her nose. "Don't take his side. I'm going."

"Fine, but your mother won't like it."

"Does she need to know every move we make?"

"According to her, yes." Terry opened MJ's door and leaned in, unbuckling his seat belt. "Let's go, little man."

MJ crossed his arms. "I told you I'm not little. I'm the tallest in my class."

Keeley smirked and opened her door, stepping onto the shoulder. *Good for you, slugger.*

"We'll be close in case you need us." Terry patted the gun Keeley knew was hidden under his suit jacket. "Your mother would also not want us to leave you."

Keeley nodded.

Brett hurried to the back and returned with an emergency first aid kit in his hands. "Come on—hurry. We have to ensure they're okay."

After confirming her son was safe and sound with Terry and Vic, Keeley followed Brett over to the injured man.

"Help me, please." He pointed toward the wrecked car. "This way."

Keeley studied the man's face. Something about his expression niggled at her. Where had she seen him before?

"I'm a paramedic," Brett said. "Where are you hurt?"

"Doesn't matter. My friend is unconscious, and I can't wake him. Help!" The man hobbled toward the crashed car.

Brett took Keeley's arm and guided her down the embankment. "Stay close."

They approached the vehicle.

Brett pointed to the leaking gas tank. "That's not good. We need to get him out."

Gas dripped onto the weeds beside the demolished vehicle. Brett rushed forward and stuck his head through the open driver's door.

Keeley stood back and observed Brett checking the man's vitals. "Is he okay?"

"His pulse is steady. Can you help me get him out of the vehicle?"

They each grasped the man under his arms, tugging backward until they were able to remove him from the car.

Brett gestured to a bunch of rocks farther down the ditch. "Quick, get him over there."

They beelined toward the area Brett had pointed out. The injured man followed.

"Keels, open the kit and hand me the smelling salts. I want to revive him."

She obeyed.

Brett waved them under his nose, and within seconds, the man's eyes flew open. He tried to sit.

Brett held him down. "Whoa, buddy. Relax. You were just in a car accident. Tell me where you hurt."

The man groaned and pointed to a deep cut on his right leg. "There." Once again, he squirmed and tried to sit.

"Coz, stay still and let him help." The other man fell to the ground and leaned forward, exposing a gun tucked into the back of his waistline.

Keeley sucked in a breath and eyed the other man.

They both turned to face her.

Two mug shots, pictured side by side, flashed into her mind. That was where she'd seen them. Their pictures were in the paper a few days ago. They were wanted fugitives—two cousins who had escaped custody after attacking and killing a young woman a few towns over.

And Keeley and Brett had just stopped to help them.

She drew in a long breath to slow her rapid heartbeat. *Stay calm.* She scooped up some gauze from his kit and fumbled with it. "Brett, can I speak with you for a minute? I need help unraveling this."

Brett raised an eyebrow.

She dipped her chin in the one man's direction, attempting to give Brett a clue.

"Sure." He stood and took her by the elbow, steering her away from the two men. "What's up?"

She held out the gauze and leaned closer, keeping up her ruse. "I've seen these guys in the news. They're the cousins who killed that young girl a few towns over. They escaped custody."

Sirens sounded in the distance.

"Good. The police can help," Brett whispered. "I'll have—"

"Seems we have us a situation here."

They turned.

The first man held his gun and gestured toward the other. "Help my cousin or I'll kill you."

Keeley glanced over her shoulder and spotted the top of her mother's bodyguards' black roof. Could she somehow signal that they needed help? They were trained professionals.

"Don't even think of it, Dr. Ash."

Keeley's gaze snapped back to the deadly fugitive.

He nodded. "That's right. We know exactly who you are."

"How?" she asked.

"The brothers told us. We was following you and wanted to toy with your minds, but little coz here went all race-car-driver crazy on me. Ended up in the ditch." He kicked his cousin's foot. "Stupid, coz. Now you've put us in a pickle."

Keeley balled her hands into fists. "Do you mean the Diglo brothers?"

"Keeley, let's just treat these men and go." Brett took the gauze from her and bandaged up the man on the ground.

Keeley knew she shouldn't press them for information, but when would she have an opportunity like this? The police would be here any minute. Plus, she could easily tap SOS on her smartwatch. Her mother had made her add the bodyguards to her emergency contact list.

The cousin with the gun snorted. "You think we're going to give away their valuable services?"

"What are you referring to? Where do these brothers operate out of? Elimac Forest?"

"How did you know that?"

Bingo.

"Petey, zip it. You've already said too much." The other cousin swatted Brett's hand away. "Never mind. Don't need your help." He sat up, then pushed himself to his feet. He limped over to his cousin and snatched the gun.

The sirens blared. Closer. Help was almost here.

"You might as well give up and tell us what operation the Diglo brothers are into." Brett waved in the direction of the sirens. "Police are here."

Petey squinted. "Wait a minute. You're the doofus who killed Eddie. You better watch your back. Horrible things are fixin' to happen. Roy's got your number."

"Who's Roy?" Keeley had to probe the men. They were holding back information.

The cousin slapped Petey on the back of the head. "You're a fool, coz. You just put a target on our backs. Now they'll never get us out of the country."

Wait—what?

Keeley swallowed to soothe her parched throat. "Do you mean that they're helping fugitives escape across the border into Alaska?"

"Now look who's gone and done it." Petey snatched the gun back, waving it in Keeley's direction. "Let's silence this redhead, shall we?"

Brett stepped in front of Keeley, raising his hands. "You better think this through. Do you really want to hurt the daughter of a Supreme Court judge?"

"Are you her boyfriend, mister?" Petey snickered.

It was time for intervention. Keeley tapped the SOS button on her smartwatch, praying that Terry or Vic would get the message.

"Look, we helped you get out of your crashed car." Brett

dangled his key fob. "Take mine. Go. We won't tell anyone you were here."

"You think we're stupid?" Petey lifted the gun higher.

Thudding sounded on the pavement.

The cousins whirled around.

Terry stood with his gun raised. "Give it up! Police are coming now. You have nowhere to run."

Petey aimed the gun toward Terry.

Brett bulldozed into him, knocking him to the ground. The gun fell into the weeds.

Terry scrambled down the embankment and hauled Petey to his feet. "Nice dive, Brett."

Brett nodded and clasped onto the other cousin just as a police cruiser arrived. "Good. Your ride is here. Now you can tell the police everything about the Diglo brothers."

Thoughts of her son so close to danger plummeted into Keeley's head. She had to get him to safety. Now. She took a step up the embankment, but movement rustling in the tall weeds behind them stopped her in her tracks.

Keeley pivoted and caught sight of two masked men dressed in camouflage gear emerging from the tree line beyond the ditch. She recognized the older brother's body type and movements from when they were in the cabin.

Before Keeley could open her mouth, the duo raised their bows, and two arrows flew in unison, hitting each of the fugitives in their chests in a perfect bull's-eye.

The cousins dropped, simultaneously.

The two men darted back into the trees.

The Diglo brothers had silenced the only witnesses Keeley had who could reveal to authorities whatever operation they hid in the forest.

NINE

Brett threw himself at Keeley, drawing her to the ground out of harm's way. "Stay down." He covered her body with his. Shouts sounded around him as Constable Jackson and another officer pursued the shooters into the woods. If there was ever a time to pray, it would be now, but Brett's stubbornness held him captive. Why couldn't he believe? He really was a doubting Thomas. *God, please help my unbelief. Why can't I trust like Keeley? Like Dad?*

Keeley pushed on his shoulders. "Can't breathe."

Brett studied the tree line to ensure the perps were gone before he rolled off Keeley. He wouldn't put her in the line of fire. Not for her sake or for MJ's.

"I need to check on MJ!" Keeley hopped up.

Terry appeared by her side, extending his hand. "Come with me, Dr. Ash."

Brett stood. "I can help her to the vehicle."

Additional sirens grew louder.

"I think you've done enough," the bodyguard barked. "You should never have stopped. You put her life and MJ's at risk. The judge won't be happy about this."

Keeley's eyes widened. "Terry! That's not true. He's a paramedic. He has an obligation to tend to the wounded." She addressed Brett. "I'll go with Terry to see MJ. You check on the cousins here. They could still be alive."

Brett highly doubted it but knew she was right.

Terry wrapped his arm around her waist as he raised his weapon. "Stay low."

They hustled up the embankment.

Something about the man's action needled Brett. Jealousy? He wanted to be the one to protect Keeley and MJ. Not some hired supposed superhero.

Brett ignored the green-eyed monster rising and dropped beside Petey, pressing two fingers on his neck.

Weak. He was still alive.

He raced to the cousin's side and checked his pulse, but the other fugitive was gone.

An ambulance stopped on the side of the road. Tina and Otto exited the vehicle.

Brett stood and waved. "Over here. This male is still alive."

The duo staggered down the ditch and ran to Brett's side.

"What's the situation?" Tina dropped her medical bag and knelt.

"Two males with arrows to the chest," Brett said. "One deceased. Petey has a weak pulse."

Otto whistled. "Arrows? That's not something you hear of every day."

"Trust me, I'm realizing these Diglo brothers are from a different breed." He faced Tina. "You met two of them yesterday."

Her mouth hung open. "Not them again. Who are they?"

Brett lifted his hands, palms up. "No idea. No one seems to know. How these brothers have managed to stay under the radar is beyond me. I'm guessing that Diglo isn't their real name."

"Identifying them will keep the police busy." Tina began her assessment of Petey's condition.

Otto radioed ahead to the coroner's office to request one to the scene.

Constable Jackson and his fellow officer emerged from the woods, approaching the group. "I've radioed for additional constables to scour the area, but the shooters are gone. It's

like they vanished into a wormhole in the vast Elimac Forest."
Jackson rubbed his brow. "It's a mystery with these guys."

"I was just telling Tina and Otto here that no one seems to
know their identity. Have you had any updates on the missing body?" Brett eyeballed the black SUV.

Terry stood leaning on the driver's side, studying the scene
below with his arms folded over his chest.

Something in his stance and glare didn't sit right with Brett.
His police training sent his tingling senses into overdrive.
Was the man simply checking out the situation or was there
another reason he intently watched the group?

"That's another mystery. The coroner has no idea how the
body disappeared, and there's no sign of it anywhere." Jackson
paused. "Video surveillance went dark for an hour on their
feed, so that didn't help the investigation. Obviously someone
who knew computers was involved."

Jackson's words silenced Brett's thoughts on the bodyguard's motives, and Brett returned his gaze to the constable. "So, a hacker?"

"Possibly." Jackson fished out his notebook. "Okay, can
you tell me exactly what happened here?"

"Sure." Brett explained the sequence of events leading up
to the crash and how they stopped to intervene, then recognized the fugitive cousins. He relayed the conversation they
had regarding some sort of operation the Diglo brothers had
in getting wanted criminals across the border.

Jackson slammed his notebook shut. "There have been reports of other fugitives seen in our area. This explains why.
Not good." He unhooked his radio. "I need to call this in and
get in touch with Hannah. Border patrol needs to be advised
of the situation."

"Good plan."

Jackson moved closer to Petey. "What's his condition?"

Tina turned. "Stable. For now. I've dressed the wound.
We're ready to transport him."

"Good," Jackson said. "I'll follow, as I want to chat with him at the hospital and get more information."

"Are we okay to leave the scene? Does Keeley need to talk to you? I'd like to get MJ back home."

"You can leave, Brett. I'll call if I need anything additional from either of you." Jackson sauntered toward the other constable, talking into his radio.

Brett faced Tina. "You good, or do you and Otto need my help?"

Otto marched toward them. "You're not on shift, so not your job."

Brett raised his hands. This paramedic did not like him. He was always sharp with him. Brett didn't understand why. "Okay, I'm leaving. Chat later."

He trudged up the incline and approached Terry. "We can leave now. I gave the constable a brief statement."

Terry pushed away from the door. "Good. You follow us. I don't want them riding with you. I've already placed MJ in his booster seat." The bodyguard didn't wait for a response and climbed into the driver's side.

Brett bit down hard on his lip to squelch the anger rising. Why did everyone seem to be against him suddenly? He just couldn't win. He grimaced and jogged to his vehicle.

Ten minutes later, he followed Keeley and MJ through the front oak doors of Olivia's estate.

"About time you got home." Olivia reached for her grandson's hand. "Time to get your teeth brushed and ready for bed, young man." She focused on Brett, wagging her finger in his face. "I will speak to you soon."

Great. Another person who wanted to ream him out.

"Mom, this wasn't his fault. He was only doing his duty of tending to the injured."

"What's your excuse? You should have told him to keep driving." Her eyes flashed. "He put you and MJ at risk."

Keeley placed her hands on her hips, standing her ground. "He did no such thing."

MJ tugged on Olivia's hand. "Gramma, I want Mr. Brett to read a story to me."

The judge's face softened. "I was going to do that tonight, love."

"No. I want him to. He read one to Mr. Harold, and his voices are funny." He scrunched his nose. "Yours aren't."

Brett covered his mouth, hiding the grin from the stoic woman as he imagined her character voices. A saying passed through Brett's head: *Out of the mouths of babes.*

Leave it to his son to speak the blatant truth.

Wait. Did he just refer to MJ as his son?

Was he admitting to himself that his father's assessment of the five-year-old was correct?

Perhaps he didn't need that DNA test after all.

His cell phone buzzed in his pocket. He removed it and checked the screen. Tina.

Why was she calling?

He raised the device. "I gotta take this. I'll read to you in a minute, MJ."

"Yay!" The boy practically bounced down the hallway.

Brett relocated to the large living room and hit Answer. "Hey, Tina. What's up?"

"Just wanted to tell you Petey didn't make it. He went into cardiac arrest, and we couldn't revive him."

No! His legs turned to jelly as his knees buckled and he plunked himself into a chair. "He was stable. What happened?"

"Not sure."

Wait—she normally didn't call him to report on their patients. "Why are you calling me?"

"Because he told me to."

What? "Why would he do that?"

"Before he went into cardiac arrest, he said to give you a message to watch your back. The Diglo brothers are coming for you. They have means everywhere to get to you. They're just waiting to lay the brother you killed to rest. Then you die. His words, not mine."

Brett drew in a sharp, audible breath. Could this day get any worse?

Now he had a target on his back.

Keeley logged her final conclusions eight days later, after scrutinizing every photograph, plant and pollen, then hit Send. She had found a specific pollen on the suspect's boots that matched the sample she'd collected near Cameron Spokene's body, linking the man to the crime scene. However, the missing suspect's body was never found, so the police could not make a positive identification, and the murder weapon still hadn't been located. Thankfully, Keeley and MJ remained safe, even though Keeley had continued on with her investigation. Her mother's bodyguards were good at what they did, and a couple of men were arrested when someone was found stalking her son's kindergarten and watching outside Keeley's college campus. Layke was unable to obtain any information from them. Their lips were shut like an uncooked clam. Someone had paid them well for their silence. They stated they were only in both areas making deliveries. Unfortunately, Layke had nothing to hold them on.

The police department suspected it was the Diglo brothers claiming their sibling's body, and after Brett revealed his conversation with Tina, they knew that to be a fact. Had the brothers taken his body to give him a proper burial, or were they trying to hide some sort of evidence? Their existence eluded everyone. Even after a full search of the woods near the cabin and the accident scene, they'd found no trace of anyone living in the area. Questions haunted Keeley's mind. Where were these brothers hiding? And why had they remained somewhat silent when they had threatened her and MJ? Brett went back to work with Layke on standby.

Brett had visited MJ on several occasions. Watching the two together warmed her heart. They were so similar. It was like looking into a mirror image in their movements and actions. Why couldn't Brett see that? He'd shared what his father said, but he still had lingering doubts. Something from his past held him back, but what?

Audrey entered the lab and plunked her briefcase on the table. "I sure hope you're ready to return to your classes. Those students are sucking the life out of me." She plopped into a chair. "How do you do it?"

Beth approached Keeley and set a coffee in front of her. "Your fave. Fuel for your upcoming class." She winked.

"Thanks." Keeley was amazed at how Beth could almost read her mind. The long hours she'd spent studying the evidence over the past week, along with being on edge that someone was watching them, had drained her energy. She required strength and alertness. Even if it came from caffeine, she'd take it.

She sipped the hazelnut coffee and addressed Audrey. "You just have to know how to handle their antics. Were they continually playing with their phones?"

"Yup."

"Didn't you make them put them in the basket on the front desk?"

She threw her hands into the air. "Now you tell me." She gestured toward Keeley's laptop. "You finish?"

"Yes. Just sent everything off to the forensics team." She held her hand toward Beth, palm facing her assistant. "Couldn't have done it without you."

They high-fived. "Teamwork. You hear anything else about the case?"

"Nothing, Beth, but I'm guessing something is brewing. The suspects have been too quiet." How much should she share with these two? "I'm concerned about Brett's safety. That threat has us all on edge. I can even sense that MJ is worried."

"Seems like he's taken a liking to Mr. Brett." Audrey put air quotes around *Mr. Brett*. "Have you told MJ yet that Brett is his father?"

"Nope. Not until Brett can commit to staying in the Yukon." She sipped again. "MJ moped for days after Preston dropped the bomb that he was breaking up with me and moving. I can't do that to my son again."

"Poor little guy." Audrey gathered her belongings and pushed off her chair. "Don't forget to back up all your evidence. You don't want it to go missing."

Keeley bristled. "Why would you say that?"

"Just because of what happened a few days ago, remember?" She pulled a list from her briefcase and tossed it on the counter. "I gotta run. You okay to teach your afternoon class? Here's the roster and where I left off."

Keeley ignored Audrey's earlier suspicious comment and brought the older woman into a hug. "Yes. Thank you for everything. I also couldn't have done this without you, either." She swallowed the thickening in her throat and willed the tears to stay away.

Audrey rubbed her back. "Love, anything for you."

The lab's landline rang, and Beth scooped up the receiver.

Keeley broke their embrace. "I better get ready for those rambunctious students. Have a great day, Audrey."

"You too, darlin'." Audrey left the room.

"Yes, she's right here." Beth held up the phone. "For you. It's the coroner. I'll go get your class set up." She handed Keeley the phone before heading out of the lab.

She took another quick sip and set down her mug. "Mrs. Faris, how are you?"

"Keeley, how many times have I told you to call me Pat?" Patricia Faris was near retirement but confessed to Keeley recently she planned to work until she reached seventy. She was married to her job.

Keeley smiled as she pictured the stout grandmother of three. "Sorry, Pat. How are you?"

"The usual. Working hard." Silence stilled the conversation. "I have news."

Something in the woman's tone told Keeley whatever she was about to say wasn't good. "Tell me." She held her breath. *Lord, give me strength.*

"You didn't hear this from me, and I'm only telling you because I know your mother is friends with the mayor and his wife. I tried to get ahold of Olivia, but she's in session right now."

"Okay."

"I've identified the skeletal remains. It's the mayor's daughter and her boyfriend."

Keeley closed her eyes, gripping the phone tighter. *Lord, no. This will break Mom's heart.* Olivia had doted on the mayor's daughter, Zoe, after she took the young woman under her wing when Zoe had shared that she wanted to become a lawyer. Something her own daughter had failed her on. "I appreciate you telling me. I'll let Mom know before the news breaks."

"Also attempting to do a DNA test just to complete the process, but the forensic artist and anthropologist did a three-dimensional reconstruction of both skulls. The mayor confirmed it's them." She clucked her tongue. "Such a shame. Zoe had a promising future as a lawyer. That girl was smart."

Keeley twirled a curl. Her mother had confirmed time and time again how smart Zoe was, to the point Keeley had become jealous of the younger woman. "Definitely a shame. I appreciate the heads-up."

"No prob. See you and your mom this Sunday at church? I missed you both last week."

Keeley loved their tight-knit community. Most of the time. Some days she wished she lived in a larger city so she could hide from prying eyes, but the community banded together when they knew one of their own required help. "Hopefully. Have a good day, Pat."

"You too. And, Keeley? Watch your back. You never know who you can trust. These hikers were murdered."

Keeley tensed. "I'm being protected, but I'll be careful."

"Good." The woman hung up.

Keeley drank more of her coffee before dialing her mother's office number. Hopefully she was out of session now, because Keeley didn't want to give her the message over a text. She tapped her thumb on the desk as she waited for her mother to pick up. *Lord, be with the mayor and his wife, Sofia.* The Coateses were a close family and did everything together. While this news gave them closure, they always had hoped Zoe would return unharmed. Somehow.

"Just getting out of court, Keeley." Her mother's breathless voice revealed her hastened movements. "What's up?"

Sweat beaded on Keeley's forehead as a rush of warmth blanketed her body. Did someone turn up the heat? She ignored the sensation and concentrated on the call. "Mom, I would rather do this in person, but I have bad news."

"Is MJ okay?"

"He's fine." Keeley inhaled. "I'm sorry to tell you the female skeleton we found was Zoe, Mom."

"No!" Grief filled her mother's one-word reply.

A wave of nausea attacked Keeley, and she swayed. *I need rest.* Her body screamed at her to take a break. "I'm so sorry, Mom. I wanted to tell you before it hit the news. I knew how close you were to Zoe."

"Yannick and Sofia will be devastated. I need to call them. See you at home." She clicked off without saying goodbye.

Figured. Her mother seemed to have more love for Zoe than her own daughter. *Harsh, Keeley. Lord, forgive me. I know what Zoe meant to Mom. Give her and the Coateses strength and comfort during this difficult time.*

Once again, dizziness plagued Keeley as sharp pains jabbed

her stomach. She gripped the sides of the table to allow it to pass. What was happening?

Approaching movement sounded, and then her lab door opened.

Brett entered.

Her knees buckled as spots blocked her vision, and another pain attacked her abdomen. Words became stuck in her throat. His voice registered in her foggy mind. She extended her hand, silently begging for help.

Brett yelled her name moments before darkness ushered her into its embrace.

TEN

Brett barreled to Keeley's side and wrapped his arms around her waist, catching her before she fell. "Keeley!" *Lord, please don't take her, too.* He gently laid her on the floor and checked her pulse, then her breathing. Both weak. He took out his cell phone and dialed 911, requesting an ambulance. He had wanted to check in on her before his night shift. Good thing he did. Was his intuition to do so from God? What had caused her fainting spell?

Her assistant ran into the room. "Keeley, where—" She halted. "No!" She fell beside her boss. "What happened?"

"No idea. I just entered the room, and she passed out. I caught her before she fell and called for an ambulance." Brett felt her forehead. "She has a fever. Not good."

"What do you think is wrong?"

"Not sure." He examined her limbs. Nothing stood out. "Has she had anything to eat or drink?"

"She had a muffin, and I brought her a coffee a bit ago." Concern shone in Beth's eyes. "Do you think it's from exhaustion? She has been working way too hard these past few days."

"Is that new for her, though? Does she normally not eat well when under deadlines?"

"Happens all the time. I've scolded her often about not looking out for herself." She clucked her tongue. "After all, she has a child to consider."

Brett racked his brain, trying to figure out the cause. "Has she fainted before?"

"No."

Brett eyed her complexion. Pale. An idea formed. "Where did the muffin come from?"

"She brought them in from home. Said she made them herself." She clutched his arm. "Wait—you think she was poisoned?"

"Possibly." Once again, he took out his phone and hit Constable Jackson's number. "Where did the coffee come from?"

"I made it." Her jaw dropped. "You don't think I poisoned her, do you?"

"I'm not saying that."

The call clicked in. "Jackson here."

"It's Brett. I'm at Keeley's lab, and I believe she's been poisoned. An ambulance is on the way." *Please save her, God. Don't let MJ lose his mama.*

Jackson barked orders in the background. "On my way with a team." He punched off.

Brett addressed Beth. "Can you find a pillow or something to cushion her head?"

She nodded and left the room.

Now for the hard call. He dialed Olivia's number and waited.

"Olivia Ash. Who's this?"

"It's Brett, Olivia."

"What do you want?" Her harsh tone seeped through the phone.

And sidelined him. Why was this woman so miserable toward him? He ignored his question and took a breath to calm his racing heartbeat. "I'm here with Keeley at her lab. She's fainted. Ambulance is—"

"What? Aren't you a paramedic? Help her!" she demanded.

Approaching sirens sounded near the campus property.

Beth returned and handed him a pillow.

Brett eased Keeley's head up and positioned the cushion underneath.

"I've examined her, and the ambulance is here now. They'll take her to Carimoose Bay Regional, if you want to meet us there. Can you get MJ, or should I pick him up?"

"No. I'm his kin. I'll get him." She disconnected.

Brett whistled and tucked his cell phone back into his pocket. "Wow, she really doesn't like me."

Beth harrumphed. "Join the crowd. She doesn't like me, either. No idea why."

"Did anyone else drink the coffee?" Brett changed the subject.

"No, it was from a coffee pod. Single serving."

Odd. How could someone have tampered with the pod? "Did you throw it out? The police will need it and her coffee mug."

"I'll get it from the garbage."

Brett hauled her back. "Wait. Let Forensics do it. They'll want to take your prints."

"You think I somehow injected a poison into her coffee pod?" Beth placed her hands on her hips.

He shook his head. "Again, I'm not saying that. The police will just want to rule out your prints because you touched the pod and her mug."

Rushed footsteps sounded in the hallway moments before Otto and another paramedic appeared.

Brett explained the situation. He then backed away, allowing them to do their job.

Constable Jackson and the forensic woman hustled into the room moments later.

"Brett, tell us what happened," Jackson said.

Brett gave them all the details, including his idea of her being poisoned. They quickly went to work bagging the evidence, dusting for prints and questioning Beth. They'd take her downtown to obtain her prints to rule her out.

The paramedics loaded Keeley onto the gurney.

"Layke, you okay if I leave with Keeley? I want to go with her to the hospital."

"Of course, Brett. We'll let you know what we find here. Ginger will check for poisons and consult with the hospital after they take a blood sample."

An hour later, Brett paced outside Keeley's hospital room. The doctor admitted her and ran a gamut of tests. Brett had called Tina to tell her he'd probably be a bit late. The older paramedic wasn't happy with him, but it couldn't be helped. Thankfully, he'd arrived at Keeley's lab hours before his shift started, or he would have had to ask for another day off.

Terry, the bodyguard, held his position beside the entrance. Feet apart, arms crossed and eyes in constant movement, scouring the area for threats. Vic lingered down the hall, watching the exits. No one was getting by these two.

The doctor emerged from Keeley's room.

Brett stepped forward. "I'm one of the paramedics on-site. Can you tell me her condition?"

He tilted his head. "You should know I can't reveal anything. You're not family."

Brett knew that but had to find out how she was doing. "Can I at least go in?"

He gestured toward the door. "You'd have to ask the almighty judge in there that question. Apparently, she's calling the shots in this hospital now. If it wasn't for her grandson, I'd have security throw her out. No one talks to me like that." He marched down the hall.

Leave it to Olivia to take over.

Brett tapped on the door and edged it open. "Okay to enter?"

MJ turned from his position at Keeley's side and raced toward him. "Yes, Mr. Brett. Come see Mama. She's sick." He took Brett's hand and dragged him into the room.

Olivia didn't have a say in the matter. Her grandson had

spoken. She sat on the opposite side of the bed, barking at someone on her phone.

Brett approached Keeley with MJ at his side. "Your mama is gonna be okay." He kept his voice low.

"I know, Mr. Brett. Jesus is on our side."

Oh, to have the faith of a child. A faith without doubts. *You once did.*

Where did that thought come from?

It was true. He had committed his life to Christ at a young age, but after tragedy struck when he was fifteen, Brett gave up on his childhood faith.

Let Him in.

His father's words from a few days ago returned. Was it time for him to come back to God and shake off his doubts?

Olivia bolted upright. "Well, you tell him if he doesn't put a rush on it, then I'll sue the entire police department." She mumbled before stuffing her phone into her purse, then turned her fiery eyes in his direction. "Who let you in?"

"I did, Gramma." MJ trotted over and tugged on the hem of her blouse. "I'm hungry. Can I have a snack?"

"I didn't bring anything."

MJ pointed to the door. "I saw chocolate bars in a case down the hall."

"I can take him there if you want, or I can stay with Keeley." Brett shifted his stance, preparing for a fight but praying she wouldn't argue in front of her grandson.

She snatched her purse. "You stay here. I need a coffee anyway." She held out her hand. "Let's go, slugger."

Brett waited until they left the room before bringing the chair closer to Keeley's side. He took her hand in his and stared at her ashen face.

A lump formed in his throat at the prospect of losing this woman—again. How had he left her so easily six years ago? His feelings for her returned, punching him in the gut. Dare he admit he had cared for her back then? They had barely known each other, but he now realized their attraction had gone deep.

What about now?

He caressed her cool face. Good—her temperature had dropped. "Come back to us, Keels. I promise I won't leave you again."

Even if he was offered the promotion in Ontario, he couldn't take it. Not now. Not when he had a family here.

He owed that to both Keeley—and his son.

His heart hitched.

Brett straightened, pressing his shoulders back as determination emerged.

He leaned forward and kissed her forehead. He would do anything to protect Keeley and MJ. Even give his own life.

Lord, catch those responsible and bring them to justice. I need my family to be safe.

Keeley labored to open her heavy eyelids. Fog crowded her mind as she scrambled to determine where she was and what had happened. She moaned and licked her sandpaper-like lips.

"Keels, can you hear me?"

Someone rubbed her hand.

Her heart hammered in her heavy chest. Why did she feel like a bulldozer had taken her out?

"Keeley, it's Brett. Can you open your eyes?" The voice grew louder.

She opened her eyes, but her cloudy vision blocked her view. She fluttered her eyelids until the room cleared.

The handsome man from her past hovered over her. "Keels. I'm here."

"Brett?" Her voice squeaked out his name. She tried to clear her throat, but it felt like she'd swallowed slivers of glass. She pointed to her neck. "Dry."

"Here, drink." He held a bent straw to her lips.

She sipped and winced as the liquid slid down her parched throat. "What…happened?"

"We think you were poisoned. I got there just as you fainted." Brett's voice shook. "Do you remember anything?"

She drank more water, allowing it to cool the fire. "I remember talking to Mom, then falling. Where was the poison?"

"We believe in the coffee. Ginger is examining the mug and the pod. The hospital has taken lots of your blood." He rubbed her arm.

"How long have I been out?"

"It's now six in the evening, so almost seven hours."

Keeley drank more water. "Where's MJ?"

"Your mom took him to get a chocolate bar from the vending machine." He chuckled. "Rather, it was MJ who took her."

Keeley tried to smile, but her lips hurt too much. "He loves chocolate."

"I gathered that." Brett caressed her face. "How are you feeling?"

"Tired. Am I dying? Is that why I feel like an elephant is sitting on my chest?" She coughed.

Brett pushed the call button. "I'm going to get the doctor in here, but they believe we got to you in time." He pointed to the IV drip. "They flushed your system and treated you."

Seconds later, the door burst open, and the medical staff entered. A man approached her bed. "Dr. Ash, I'm Dr. Garrison. How are you feeling?" He placed his fingers on her wrist.

The nurse checked the machines.

"Chest is heavy. Tired. Am I dying?" She repeated her earlier question to Brett.

Dr. Garrison patted her arm. "All indications are showing improvement, so we believe you're going to be fine. Someone was looking out for you, young lady."

"Have they determined the poison used?"

Dr. Garrison turned toward Brett. "Wait. I remember now where I know you from. You're the newer paramedic."

"Brett Ryerson. Friend of Keeley's." He extended his hand.

The doctor returned the gesture. "Nice to meet you, but I still can't discuss her condition."

"Doc, it's okay. Brett was the one who found me. If it wasn't for him, I'd probably be dead." She drank more water before continuing. "Please tell us."

"Well, we won't know exactly until our lab speaks with the police." He chortled. "However, if your mother has anything to do with it, we should know soon. I've heard she's putting on the pressure."

"Yeah, she tends to do that. Sorry." In this case, Keeley didn't mind her mother's interference.

The doctor finished his assessment. "Your vitals are improving. That makes me happy."

"Her color is returning, too." Brett smiled at her. "That's also a good sign."

Keeley absentmindedly reached to smooth her hair. "I'm sure I look a fright."

"You're as gorgeous as ever, Keels." Brett kissed her forehead, then backed away quickly. "Sorry."

"You don't—"

The door opened, and MJ bounded toward the bed. "Mama!"

Her mother ended her phone call and approached. "How are you feeling?"

How many times would she be asked that today? "I'm tired."

MJ stood on the bed railing, drawing himself upward.

The doctor held him back. "Just a minute, young man. Your mother still needs rest."

"It's okay, Doc." Keeley patted a spot beside her. "He's all the medicine I need right now."

MJ crawled onto the bed and nestled himself close to Keeley.

"Okay, but they will have to leave soon." He gestured toward the nurse. "We'll leave you alone now. I'll check on you a bit later, okay?"

"Thanks, Doc."

The doctor and nurse left the room.

Keeley wrapped her arm around MJ and kissed his cheek. "Love you, slugger."

"Wuf you, too, Mama." MJ rested his head on Keeley's chest.

A knock sounded moments before the door opened and Layke stuck in his head. "Can we come in?"

Keeley wasn't sure how much longer she'd be able to keep her eyes open, but she waved him in. "Of course."

Layke entered, followed by Ginger.

"We have news and thought you'd want to know."

Keeley's mother stood from where she'd been sitting. "Have you completed your tests yet?"

MJ squirmed in Keeley's arms.

She winced at her mother's use of her judge voice when she'd asked the question. "Mom."

Ginger raised her hand. "It's okay. She's already proved how far her gavel and wallet reach."

"Mom, please take MJ for a walk." She didn't want her son to hear what the police were about to say. "Go with Gramma, slugger."

He pouted. "I want to stay here."

That sad face is hard to resist. Keeley suppressed a grin. "It will only be for a few minutes. How about you get Mama some chips, okay?"

His eyes sparkled. "Me too?"

"No. You can have some of mine." Not that Keeley wanted anything to eat right now, but her son didn't need to know that. She grazed her lips on his forehead. "How does that sound?"

"Good!" He hopped down from the bed. "Let's go, Gramma."

Her mother scowled but took MJ's hand before exiting.

"Go ahead, Ginger. Tell me what you found." Keeley gripped her hospital bedsheets tighter, bracing for the forensic investigator's news.

Ginger took out her notebook and read from it. "The poison wasn't in the coffee but on the rim of your mug."

Brett whistled. "Wow, that's a new one. What poison?"

"Highly concentrated privet."

"What?" Was it a coincidence that Keeley was poisoned by a plant? Was someone sending her a message? "That plant isn't found in the Yukon."

"I'm thinking that whoever did this was only trying to scare you. This plant doesn't normally kill." Ginger tucked her notebook back into her pocket. "We tested all the mugs in your lab, and yours was the only one with privet on it."

"Did you always drink from the same cup?"

She pictured the World's Greatest Mama mug. "Yes, Layke, mostly. MJ gave it to me for Mother's Day last year."

Layke withdrew his notepad and handed it to her. "I'm gonna need the names of everyone in your department who'd have access to your lab and lunchroom."

"Do you really think it was someone I work with? Lots of folks come and go in my lab." Her fingers shook as she took the pen. The thought of having to name all her precious colleagues tore at her heart. It felt like a betrayal. A tear slipped down her cheek.

Brett grazed her arm. "It's okay. It may not be one of them."

Her gaze snapped to his, her heart lodging in her ribs from his gentleness. How did he know her thoughts?

His cell phone buzzed, and he looked at his screen. "Tina again. I gotta get to work." He pocketed his phone and focused on her. "You rest. I'm on the night shift. I'll be back early in the morning."

She nodded, words wedged in her throat.

"Constable, I realize Olivia has bodyguards outside the door, but they'll probably leave when MJ does, as they're tasked to protect him. Can you have someone keep watch over Keeley?"

"Of course, Brett."

"I'm concerned that when whoever did this realizes Keeley didn't die, they'll try again in some other form."

Keeley didn't miss Brett's tone. Her stomach fluttered at

the thought of him caring, but she also realized the danger wasn't over. The question was—when and where would this person try again?

"Sorry again for being late earlier." Brett jumped into the back of the ambulance he shared with Tina, his thoughts still on Keeley. Constable Jackson had promised to protect her, but Brett wanted badly to stay by her side. He wasn't a police officer any longer, but he still felt responsible for keeping her safe. He and Tina had been dispatched multiple times throughout the night. Brett was ready for this busy shift to be over.

"You already apologized." Tina refilled the cabinets with supplies, getting ready for their next call. "It's clear you care for the woman."

Was he that obvious, and when had his feelings leapfrogged into something more than friendship? *Face it, you're smitten.* "Yeah, I guess I do."

"Her son is a cutie."

He reached for the cabinet door, but his hand stopped in midair. Where had she seen MJ? Suspicion crawled up his spine. "Have you met MJ somewhere?"

She looked down, concentrating her efforts on restocking supplies. "I saw him at that accident you helped with."

How could she have? He was in the back seat of the body-guards' tinted SUV. "But how—"

The buzzer blared throughout the garage moments before 911 dispatched their ambulance to a woman in labor on the bridge over Elimac Lake.

Their conversation and Brett's suspicions would have to wait. For now. "Let's go." He hopped from the back and darted around to the driver's side.

Nine minutes later, Brett drove onto the bridge separating Carimoose Bay and the nearest town.

A car sat at the top, the driver's door open. Streetlights illuminated the area and revealed a man waving his hands, beckoning to them.

Brett parked behind the red vehicle and jumped out, leaving the lights fixed on the car.

Trucks barreled onto the opposite end, parking nose to nose, blocking anyone from either exiting or coming onto the bridge.

Tina caught his arm. "What's going on?"

Two more trucks pulled onto the other end, parking in the same position.

Trapped with nowhere to run.

The man beside the car shoved a balaclava down over his face and pointed a rifle in their direction. "Time for you to pay, Mr. Paramedic."

Men on both sides of the bridge leaped from their trucks. All masked and dressed in hunting gear, rifles attached to their shoulders.

One approached. "Mama says our mourning time is over. Time for you to pay for killing our little brother." He turned to the others.

Bile burned the back of Brett's throat as terror seized every muscle in his body. He dropped his medical bag.

"Brett, they're gonna kill us." Tina's forced words revealed her apprehension.

Lord, what do I do?

Brett stepped in front of his partner. "It's me you want. Let her go."

"Sorry, she's collateral damage. Don't worry—Keeley and MJ are next. This time we'll succeed. Don't think those bodyguards or her judge mother can keep them safe at that hospital."

Brett's legs weakened, and he stumbled but caught himself. *Lord, protect my family!*

The hunter peeked over his shoulder. "Time to do this."

One man stood guard with his rifle trained on Brett and Tina while the other members climbed onto their truck's cargo bed, then removed dirt bikes.

They sped off the bridge, but one driver stopped and dis-
mounted.

It was then Brett noted multiple bags close to where they
left their abandoned vehicle.

No! They were going to blow up the bridge with Brett and
Tina on it.

The man held up a device. "Fire in the hole!"

"Jump!" Brett grabbed his partner's hand and charged to
the other side of the bridge, catapulting over the railing.

He plunged into the dark water feetfirst and prayed Tina
had done the same thing.

Their lives depended on it.

ELEVEN

Brett emerged from the icy waters and gulped in a breath, struggling to see in the darkness. He treaded water, circling to find his partner. "Tina!" he yelled as water gushed into his mouth. He spit it out, inhaled and submerged again with his eyes open, searching for her. The murky waters inhibited his hunt for Tina, so he broke to the surface again. He finally spotted her a few feet away. Brett swam quickly to her location and towed her face up to the river's edge and onto the rocky shore.

Brett checked her vitals.

She wasn't breathing.

"No!" Brett cleared her airway and gave her rescue breaths, then compressions. Without his equipment, he had to administer CPR the old-fashioned way.

He repeated the process. "Come on, Tina! Talk to me."

She coughed, spewing out water.

Brett rolled her onto her side, allowing the rest to expel. "Thank God. I thought I lost you." He helped her to sit up. "You okay?"

"I will be." She breathed in and out multiple times.

Brett pushed himself upright and scanned the area to ensure the Diglo brothers had left the vicinity.

All was quiet. For now.

"Can you walk? We need to get through those woods and onto the highway to flag someone down."

She nodded, holding out her hand.

He helped her stand, wrapping his arm around her waist. Any earlier suspicions about Tina dissipated. She wouldn't have put her own life on the line if she was one of them.

Would she? Or was she good at deception?

Together, they stumbled through the dark woods to the side of the highway. Brett gestured toward a boulder. "Lean on that. I hear some traffic, and I'm going to check it out."

She sat. "Make sure it's not them!"

Brett hid behind a tree and listened for dirt bikes. When no rumbles sounded, he stole a glimpse at the road. Headlights approached from around the bend. Without daylight, he couldn't make out the vehicle, but he had to take a risk. He stepped out and waved his hands, praying the driver was a friend, not a foe.

The van stopped, and a woman rolled her window down, eyeing his soaked clothing. "Are you all right?"

"Yes. Do you have a cell phone? I need to call 911. Accident ahead and the bridge—out." He realized his garbled words probably didn't make sense. *Calm down, Brett.* But he had to get to Keeley and MJ. Their lives were in danger.

Her head turned, and she pointed.

He followed her line of vision.

Smoke billowed upward toward the starry sky, confirming his statement regarding the bridge.

The woman fished in her purse and passed him the phone. "Here. Let me pull to the side."

"Thank you for being a Good Samaritan." He dialed 911 and requested emergency services at his location.

Forty minutes later, after getting checked and cleared by Otto, a constable agreed to take him to the hospital once he explained the situation. They followed the ambulance as Otto rushed Tina to be checked by doctors.

Brett hopped from the cruiser as soon as the constable parked. He sprinted through the double doors toward the stairs, taking the steps two at a time to get to Keeley's room in the ICU. He couldn't wait for the constable or the elevators.

Reaching her floor, he ran down the corridor and stumbled into her room.

Only to find it empty. They had changed the bedsheets. No sign of Keeley.

Where was she? Brett wiped his sweaty palms on his pants, then raced toward the nurses' station. He slapped his hand on the counter.

The nurse glanced up from her screen. "Calm down, sir." Her eyes traveled over his dirty, wet uniform. "You're a paramedic. You should know better. Now, how can I help?"

Brett, relax. He inhaled. "Where's the patient in room 204?"

"Are you family?"

"No, but I was just with her last evening." He realized he was breaking protocol, but he had to find her.

The doctor from earlier walked around the corner. "Brett, you're back. Keeley has improved, and we needed the bed in ICU, so we moved her to the fourth floor."

"Thank you. What room?"

"Jill? Tell him. The patient would want him to know." He snickered. "Trust me, you don't want the judge's wrath. She just arrived with her grandson."

Already? It's still early. Clearly, Olivia had made quite the reputation in under twenty-four hours.

The nurse tapped the computer keys. "Room 408."

"Thank you." Brett turned to the doctor, a plan forming in his mind. "Is she stable enough to be discharged into my care this morning? As you know, I'm a paramedic."

"Well, she's stronger, but I wouldn't recommend it." He tilted his head. "What's this about?"

Brett leaned in and lowered his voice. "Her life has been threatened, and she's too accessible here."

"Even with her buffed bodyguards?" He laced his words with sarcasm.

"I just barely escaped from the men who are after her. I

need to get her to a secure location." Brett's police lingo returned in a flash.

"Well, you would need her authorization." He hesitated. "And probably the judge's."

"Okay, we'll be in touch." Brett raced to the exit, pushed the door open and bounded up the stairs two more floors. He skidded to a stop after entering the corridor and spied the bodyguards. He headed toward them.

They eyed his crumbled, damp uniform and stood side by side, blocking the entrance.

"What happened to you?" Terry crossed his arms in his normal protective stance.

"Long story. Listen, Keeley and MJ are in danger." Brett had to tell her the plan. "I need to see her right away."

They looked at each other.

"Come on, guys. I wouldn't harm either of them." Brett raked his fingers through his dirty hair.

Terry opened the door. "We're watching." He sniffed. "Take a shower, man."

Brett ignored them and hurried into the room. "Keels, we have to leave."

Her eyes widened, and she sat straighter in bed. "What happened?"

Olivia rose to her feet, took one look at Brett and grabbed MJ's hand. "Slugger, let's go for a walk."

Brett motioned toward the door. "Be sure to take either Terry or Vic with you. Leave one at the door."

Olivia pursed her lips and nodded at Brett before exiting with her grandson.

"We need to get you discharged and back behind your mother's guarded estate." Brett hated the distress coming out in his breathless words.

"Tell me what's going on." She reached for him.

He took her hands in his. "Tina and I were targeted on the Elimac Bridge. The Diglo brothers told me I had to pay for killing their little brother, and he said you and MJ were next." He explained how they blew up the bridge moments before he and Tina launched into the water.

Her eyes widened. "Are you okay?"

"Bruised from hitting the water, but Tina almost didn't make it." He rubbed his brow. "I had to resuscitate her."

Keeley's mouth formed an O.

"How are you feeling? Did you get a good rest?" Her regular peachy skin tones encouraged Brett.

"Much better but tired." She raised her arm. "They still have me hooked up to an IV."

"I spoke to the doctor. He said you were improving. I realize I'm not a doctor, but I'm trained, so he may discharge you to my care. If you and your mother agree, of course." Brett resisted the urge to roll his eyes.

"Yeah, she yelled at him earlier." Keeley swung her legs over the edge. "I'm feeling stronger, but do you think it's wise for me to leave so soon?"

"We need to get you out of the hospital. The Diglo brothers know you're here. They've targeted you, MJ and me." Brett wasn't sure how she'd take the next news, but he had to be honest. "Keels, we all need protection, and the safest place right now is in your mother's gated community. We have to lie low for a while, including your mother."

Panic twisted Keeley's facial muscles. "But what about your father?"

Brett's shoulders slumped. *Good question.* How could he protect them and spend time with his father? *Lord, I need to do both.* "I will check with Nancy to see how he's doing. It should only be for a few days. Hopefully."

"My mother won't like it, but at least we have her bodyguards."

Brett recalled his earlier suspicions of Terry's behavior. "Do you trust Terry and Vic?"

"I don't have any reason not to. Why?"

"Just a vibe I get from Terry." He tapped his chin. "Nothing I can put my finger on at the moment. Your mother should take a leave of absence from the courts, too. Stay out of the limelight."

Keeley grasped Brett's arm. "You don't think they'll come after her, do you?"

"We can't take any risks. Will she agree? I know she doesn't like me."

"She'll have to." Keeley rang the call bell. "I'm going to get the doctor here so they can start my discharge."

"I'll make some calls once I get a new phone." Brett walked to the large window and peered into the parking lot. Dark clouds had blanketed the sky and blocked the rising sun, ushering an eeriness into the region. "When are you going to tell your mom?"

The door opened. "Tell me what?" Olivia and MJ returned.

Keeley stepped into slippers by her bed and approached. "Mom, Brett thinks we all need to sequester ourselves in your gated home." A pause. "Including you. No court appearances. Nothing."

"Really? Yay!" MJ bounced on his tippy-toes.

At least one of them was excited.

Olivia placed her hands on her hips and turned to Brett, eyes glaring. "You come back into her life, and you think you can just take over? My daughter and grandson are my responsibility, not yours. How dare—"

"Mom. Stop." Keeley's tone halted the conversation. "Brett is only trying to help. We're doing this."

Olivia positioned herself in Brett's personal space and waggled her finger at him. "If her condition worsens, I will hold you personally responsible. You hear me?"

Loud and clear.

There was no denying the judge's hammer would come down hard if Brett put her family in danger. He didn't know which was worse—facing the Diglo brothers or the wrath of Chief Justice Olivia Ash.

* * *

Keeley shuffled into the kitchen early the next morning, willing strength into her weary body. She was happy to be in her own bed but still perplexed on who would use plants to poison her. The Diglo brothers seemed to be more of the hunting type. They used knives, rifles and arrows for their kills. Not weeds. She also wanted to do more research on the Yukon's plant life. The doctor thought Keeley had only ingested a small portion of the poisonous weed, and that was why she didn't die. *Thank You, God. Tell me, who would do this?* She refused to think any of her coworkers would betray her. No, it had to be someone else. Many had passed through her labs for tours—law enforcement, coroners, students, doctors, to name a few.

Keeley reached into the cupboard for a mug but hesitated. Could someone have gotten into her mother's kitchen? Surely not. Her mother had the best security at her residence. However, Keeley wasn't taking any chances, so she vigorously washed all the mugs before grinding beans and brewing a large pot of hazelnut coffee.

She took her mug and nestled into her favorite chair in the sunroom to catch the sunrise. She loved watching the colors change as the sun peeked over the mountains. Yesterday's dark clouds had produced strong winds, hail and rain, but had passed quickly. Keeley pictured MJ snuggled in Brett's lap last night to take shelter from the sound of hail pinging on the windows. MJ hated storms.

She smiled as she placed her lips on the rim of her coffee cup. *Lord, I could get used to picturing that sweet sight of MJ being rocked by his father.*

A sunray bounced off the mountainside, sending a line of illumination on the treetops. Perhaps a sign of things to come? She prayed it would happen. Her feelings for Brett had sneaked up on her, and she found herself dreaming of a life together with MJ and Brett—one happy family.

Was that possible?

Not if her mother had any say in Keeley's love life. Her mom hated that they made her postpone all her court proceedings, but Brett had told them about his conversation with the older brother on Elimac Bridge. He was coming for all of them. Brett had negotiated a week off from his job and would check in on his father every day. Vic would escort him there and back.

The arrangement was perfect.

At least, she prayed it was.

"You're up early." Brett approached from the opposite door.

She flinched and placed her hand on her chest. "You scared me."

"Sorry. How are you feeling?"

"Coming along. Felt good to sleep in my own bed." She took a sip of coffee before raising her cup. "Don't worry—I scrubbed all the mugs. They're safe. Grab some and join me."

"Will do. I have news from Constable Jackson." He left and returned within two minutes, sitting in the chair next to her. "Magnificent view."

"The best. I love God's handiwork. Look at those colors." She stole a peek at his profile.

His tightened jaw revealed his angst.

She remembered he didn't like to talk about God. "Why do you find it hard to trust God?"

His gaze tore from the sunrise to her within seconds. "Because He took too much from me."

She reached over and settled her hand on his arm. "Tell me."

His previously peaceful face morphed into a haunted, tortured expression. He rested his head back. "Well, for one thing, an escaped convict murdered my mother. God could have stopped it but chose not to."

Her jaw dropped. "I'm so sorry. I didn't know that."

"I just don't understand why He allows His children to go through so much pain. It's like stumbling through the wilderness, not knowing which direction to go sometimes."

"So, you made a commitment at one point?"

"Yes, as a boy. And then…" He took a sip.

"Then what?" She hated to probe but, at the same time, knew if he talked it out, perhaps it would help.

"I'd rather not say."

Secrets. She had enough of those with her tight-lipped mother.

He fished out his cell phone from his jeans pocket. "We're going to have a meeting today."

Misdirection. Obviously that was the end of their God talk. "What type of meeting?"

"Constable Jackson texted me. They've been looking into the growing number of fugitives spotted in the area. He's bringing his wife, Hannah, to talk to us about it."

"It will be good to see her again. But why us? We're not law enforcement." Keeley finished her coffee and set her mug on the glass end table in between their chairs.

"Well, Layke knows my background and wanted to report on what they found regarding the two fugitives we talked to at the accident. Thought maybe something would stand out to us." Brett leaned toward her. "Are you up for a visit?"

"Of course. What time?"

He checked his watch. "Nine. Is that okay? I can make it later if you want." He set his phone beside her discarded cup.

She hopped to her feet. "That's fine. I just need to go make myself more presentable."

"You look great so soon after being poisoned." He winked. "In fact, *gorgeous* would be the word I'd use."

She huffed. "Hardly. I also want to check my emails." She pointed to the kitchen. "There's lots to eat."

"What about MJ?"

"We're keeping him away from kindergarten, too. I should get him up, though."

Brett pushed himself upright. "Can I do it? I love spending time with him."

"Of course." She crossed her arms, tilting her head. "Do you believe me that he's your son now?"

"I'm getting there, but it's hard when…"

Once again, he let his sentence drop.

More secrets?

His phone flashed as a text appeared on the screen.

Keeley caught the note before it disappeared.

The promotion is yours, if you want it. Come back to Ontario.

Keeley stiffened every muscle in her weary body. *He's leaving*. What was the point in even trying to get close to him again? No, she couldn't let him back into their lives. "Never mind. I'll get my son ready." She marched down the hall and up the stairs to MJ's room. She hated to act like a two-year-old going through a tantrum, but she couldn't help it.

Just when she thought they'd made a breakthrough, the imaginary wall became impenetrable.

And she wouldn't let her son get hurt again.

Even though she realized it was probably already too late.

TWELVE

Brett studied the text from his former supervisor in Ontario. Had Keeley's sudden shift in mood been because she'd seen the message regarding the promotion? *She thinks you're leaving. Tell her. Tell her you're staying.*

Could he? The question was…did she *want* him to stay? He wrestled with his internal thoughts, bouncing back and forth like a Ping-Pong ball. But he knew in his heart he wouldn't leave when he wanted to be involved in MJ's life—even if that meant Keeley didn't want to further a relationship with him.

The front gate buzzed on Olivia's security monitor system, interrupting his fluctuating thoughts.

Vic appeared around the corner and clicked a button. "You know these folks?" He pointed to the screen.

Brett stood and walked over, leaning in to get a better look. "Yes, that's Constable Layke Jackson and his wife, Hannah. They're here to see Keeley and me. Please let them in."

Vic shook his head. "They're not on the list."

"List? What list?" Brett scrunched up his nose.

"Judge Ash's. No one gets in unless approved by her."

Shuffling feet sounded behind them, and Brett pivoted.

Keeley appeared dressed in a green-and-navy plaid tailored shirt and jeans. "Since when does my mother have this supposed list?"

"Since you made us sequester ourselves in her home." He

held up his tablet. "If they're not on the list, they're not allowed in."

"That's absurd. These people are here to help with the case so we can all get on with our lives." Keeley pushed Vic aside and hit the button to open the gate.

Brett held in a chuckle. Seemed Keeley found the strength to get by the bodyguard. *Good on you, Keels.*

Vic scowled. "Fine, you can answer to your mother. Not me. I'm adding that in my notes." He keyed on his tablet before marching down the hall.

"Wow. Your mother does rule the roost." Brett squeezed her shoulder. "Listen, I wanted to tell you—"

The doorbell chimed.

"I gotta get that." She hurried down the hardwood corridor.

A couple of minutes later, after they greeted the guests, the group sat at the dining room table.

Brett's knee bounced in anticipation of what news Layke and Hannah had to share. His childhood nervous habit of shaking his leg had followed him into adulthood, and he hated it. Brett placed his hand on his knee to settle his nerves.

"Hannah, how are you feeling? You must be due soon."

Hannah rubbed her protruding belly. "Three weeks, but this baby has been kicking up a storm, Keeley. I think he or she is trying to break free of my womb."

Keeley laughed. "How's Gabe?"

"Excited to meet his baby sister or brother." She squeezed Jackson's hand. "Daddy is, too."

"Sure am." Jackson cleared his throat. "Let's get down to it. I spoke to Hannah regarding the conversation you had with the fugitives."

"Did you find out their names?" Brett asked.

"Yes. Peter and Tom Lees. They were both convicted of murder and escaped custody during prison transport." Jackson opened a file folder he'd brought. "Also, the arrow tips were laced with privet."

Keeley gasped. "So, my attack and this one are connected. Do you think it's the Diglo brothers?"

"That's our conclusion." Jackson turned to Hannah. "Tell them what you discovered."

"Yesterday, we caught a fugitive trying to cross the border. He was driving erratically toward US customs, so we stopped him before he could get there. His behavior was suspicious, even though his documentation didn't raise a red flag, so we went through his car." Hannah dragged Jackson's folder closer. "The man's real name is Willy Carson, but that's not what his passport said. When he changed his car registration, he forgot to change his insurance."

"Obviously, a convict not firing on all cylinders," Jackson said. "After an intense interrogation with both Hannah's border patrol officers and us, he finally confessed to the Diglo brothers helping him. He said they were extremely dangerous and scared even him."

Brett leaned back. "That's why you're telling us this. Since they're targeting us."

Jackson shifted in his chair. "Yes. We don't normally share information with civilians, but I know your background, and we want you to be very cautious. We're doing everything we can to find the Diglos."

"Did they tell you who these brothers are?"

Hannah lifted her index finger. "I can answer that, Keeley. I was in the interrogation. Willy said he didn't know their real identities. Apparently, they only referred to each other using initials in front of him. They blindfolded him so he didn't know where their operation was located, only that he could hear lots of nature around him." She made air quotes with the word *nature*.

"Probably the forest." Keeley twirled a curl.

Hannah nodded. "That's my guess, too. He also said they provided all his new documentation."

"Keeley, was there anything that stood out in your time

with them?" Layke steepled his fingers and placed his elbows on the table.

"Well, I only met two of them, and the older brother definitely seemed to be the one in charge. They referred to a woman as well. Could that be the leader of the organization?"

"Possibly." Jackson pointed to the paper in the file. "Tell them what else you found, Hannah."

"Okay, your coffee mug and the arrows were laced with privet, and that doesn't grow in the Yukon. So they're importing it somehow." Hannah flipped a page in the folder. "One of our officers stopped a van the other day and found privet seeds hidden among other plant life. The driver confessed he was only delivering them to a certain warehouse, but when we looked into it further, the location was bogus."

Brett leaned forward. "You have no idea where it was actually going?"

"Correct."

"So, if we find where the privet is being grown, we find those responsible." Brett rubbed his tense neck muscles.

"Agree," Jackson said. "We have teams searching surrounding forests. So far, nothing has surfaced."

"I appreciate you sharing this information." Keeley slumped in her chair.

Hannah shifted positions, and her hand flew to her abdomen. "Baby's kicking." She turned to Brett. "One more thing before we go. Mr. Carson also said something that stood out to me. He said that he was in the room when the brothers were making plans to retarget a paramedic since they had failed to kill him on the bridge."

"They know you're still alive, Brett. You both need to watch your back." Jackson closed the folder. "We're increasing patrols in this area to help. Don't leave the house for now."

Once again, Brett's knee bounced, his blood pressure rising. "I need to check on my father. I'm not sure how much longer he has."

"I understand. Be sure to take a bodyguard with you." Jackson stood. "Rest assured, we're doing everything we can to find these men. We'll brief you with anything new."

Brett rose and extended his hand. "Thanks so much."

After the group left, Brett called Nancy to get an update on his father. She'd reported that he had rallied and was now eating again. That news brought joy to his heart. Perhaps God was finally listening.

Maybe.

Brett pocketed his phone before joining Keeley and MJ in the kitchen. He leaned on the door frame and observed MJ making himself a peanut-butter-and-jam sandwich. Keeley had her back to him as she reached for something in the fridge. MJ loaded the knife with jam, and it plopped onto the floor.

"Rats." He dropped the knife, and his hand flew to his mouth.

Keeley turned. "Michael Joshua, what did I tell you about using that word?"

"Sorry, Mama." His puppy-dog eyes caught Brett's gaze and widened as if silently pleading for help.

Brett subdued the laughter bubbling inside and entered the room. "Here, let me help." He snatched up the dishcloth and wiped the jam from the floor. "I'll show you how I used to make PB&J sandwiches."

"Okay." MJ stood on his tippy-toes.

"First, take some peanut butter." Brett put some on the knife. "Then slather one piece of bread."

"Slather?"

Keeley chuckled. "He's five, Brett. That's a big word."

"How about *spread*?"

"Oh." MJ dipped his finger into the jam jar and stuck it in his mouth.

"Son, you know Gramma's rules." Keeley's lips curved slightly upward.

Brett guessed she was trying to contain the same laughter as him. He grabbed a spoon and dipped it into the jar. "Okay, now add a little jam to a spoon, because you should never mix the two."

MJ tilted his tiny head. "Why?"

"That's just a rule in every kitchen, right, Keels?"

"Especially this one." She folded her arms. "Gramma hates that. Believe me, I learned the hard way."

"What's next, Mr. Brett?"

He placed the other piece of bread to the left of the one containing the peanut butter. "Add the jam here." He held up his index finger. "Never put one on top of the other. It's a Ryerson household rule." He added the jam.

"But why?"

Brett's gaze shifted to Keeley. "You know, I'm not sure." He set the spoon down and picked up the two slices. "Now you put them together, and voilà—the best PB&J sandwich you'll ever have." He handed it to MJ, winking at Keeley.

She giggled like a schoolgirl.

A sound he loved.

MJ took his sandwich, sat at the table and bowed his head. "Thank You, God, for this food. Amen." He stuffed the bread into his mouth.

Brett's jaw dropped. The way MJ had folded his hands reminded him of when he was a kid. Brett would position both index fingers into a steeple and bring his hands together.

Just like MJ.

Keeley's phone dinged. She withdrew it from her jeans pocket and swiped the screen. "That's odd."

He turned back to her. "What is it?"

"The coroner just sent me an email to my personal account. She doesn't have that address." She tapped on her phone and read. "What? Impossible."

Keeley swayed and dropped into a chair.

Brett moved beside her. "What does the email say?"

She glanced at MJ and then back to Brett, turning the phone in his direction. "Read this." She kept her voice soft.

Brett leaned closer for a better view.

Olivia,
Hey, friend. Tried to reach you by phone but couldn't. I'm sure Keeley would have given you the news of your daughter by now. My deepest condolences for the passing of Zoe. Please let me know if there's anything you need. See you at our next function.
Pat

Brett scrolled and continued to read. "Zoe was your mother's daughter? That means—"

Keeley straightened, her eyes hardening. "Zoe was my half sister, and my mother has been lying to me all my life."

Not the way Brett thought this day would go.

Keeley closed her hands into impregnable fists as her pulse zinged. *How could you keep this a secret, Mom?* She inhaled a long breath, exhaling slowly. She must calm down before she approached her mother.

Zoe was my sister? Mom, there's no coming back from this one.

"Wait. She said Olivia." Brett handed her phone back. "Did she email you by mistake?"

"Looks that way. When I was a teenager, Mom and I thought it would be cute to have matching emails, except using different numbers. I picked ashtree17. Mom picked ashtree19. They're close, so an easy mistake." Keeley tucked her phone away. "I thought she got rid of that email address. I only use mine when I don't want anything to go to my work email."

MJ approached, interrupting their quiet conversation. "Mr. Brett, that PB&J sandwich was delicious." MJ took his plate to the sink.

"See, I told you, sport. Only way to make one."

"What did I tell you about eating fast, young man?" Keeley pushed herself up to a standing position. "Brett, can you keep him occupied? I need to go have a little chat with my mother."

He nodded. "Sure, but maybe you should wait until you've calmed a bit."

"Yeah, I thought so, too, but I'm afraid that would take too long." Keeley marched from the room and crossed the wide corridor, making her way to Chief Justice Olivia Ash's home office.

She tapped on the door before pushing it open. "Mom, we need to talk."

Her mother turned from her position by the window and wiped a tear away. She rolled her shoulders as if composing herself. "Listen, Sofia, I need to go," she said into her cell phone. "Seems that my daughter has something to say. Chat later."

She strode over to her desk and tossed her phone on top. "What did I tell you about not entering my office before I gave you permission?"

Keeley gripped her phone tighter and strode up to her mother. "Tell me something. Why didn't you let me know I had a sister?"

Her mother's blue eyes widened as she dropped into her desk chair. "What—how?"

The normally well-versed judge stumbled over her words.

Keeley placed her cell phone on her mother's desk. "Seems an email from Pat offering her condolences on the passing of your daughter Zoe came to me by mistake. Were you ever going to tell me?" She refrained from subduing the anger in her voice. She just couldn't help it.

Her mother read the email before slouching back in her high-back desk chair. "I'm sorry."

Heat coiled around Keeley's spine, raising her temperature. "You're sorry? Sorry you were caught? Mom, you had an affair with the mayor, and now you're best friends with his wife?" She placed her hands flat on her mother's desk and leaned forward. "After all the times you've chastised me. How could you?"

Her mother's lips trembled. "It was a mistake that happened when you were one." She pointed to the chair across from her desk. "Sit. It's time you knew."

You think? Man, she had to curb her foul mood. She plopped into the chair, crossing her arms and legs. "I'm listening."

Her mother poured herself a glass of water from the pitcher at the side of her desk. "Yannick and Sofia were close friends of your father's and mine. Yannick suggested I go to a seminar in Vancouver. He was going and thought it would be beneficial to my career."

Keeley guessed where her mother's story was heading.

"Your father didn't want me to go. Joshua said you wouldn't do well without me. You were a—"

"I know—a very colicky baby. You've thrown that in my face many times."

"Please let me finish. Joshua and I had a huge fight when I told him I had to go. My career depended on it. He disagreed." She drank her water. "If he'd had his way, I would've been a stay-at-home mom. Not that there's anything wrong with that. It just wasn't for me." Another sip. "We hadn't been getting along very well, so I went anyway. Yannick was right. The conference was a career changer. We spent long hours in sessions during the day, and in the evenings, we went out together for dinners. We both were having marital struggles. You can guess what happened. One night. One mistake."

"That's how it can happen." Who was Keeley to judge? However, she hadn't been married. "What did you do when you found out you were pregnant?"

"I confessed. Everything." She exhaled loudly. "Your father was livid and—"

Keeley uncrossed her legs and leaned forward, elbows to knees. "That's when he had his heart attack, wasn't it?"

Sadness passed over her mother's normally stoic face. "Yes," she whispered.

Fury scorched Keeley's cheeks. Her mother had contributed to her father's death. *Unforgivable.* "You caused his heart attack? Mom, how could you? You stole my father from me." Keeley gripped the armchair until her fingers went numb.

Her mother waggled her finger in Keeley's direction. "I did no such thing. I found out later your father had a heart condition we didn't know about and that his heart attack was only a matter of time."

Keeley huffed and slumped back in the chair. "But, Mom, why wouldn't you keep Zoe? I don't understand."

Her mother got up and meandered to the window. "I was an instant single mother, stressed and striving to become a Supreme Court judge. I had a reputation to uphold."

"So, you placed your precious career over your unborn child? What did you tell Yannick?"

Her mother fiddled with the blind cords. "That I would somehow hide the pregnancy and put the baby up for adoption."

"But he wouldn't let you, right?"

"No. He confessed everything to Sofia. Needless to say, she was angry, but over the next few weeks, she told Yannick she wanted to raise the child." She turned from the window. "Sofia couldn't get pregnant, and she said even though she hated the fact we had an affair, she felt Zoe was a gift to her, kind of like Hagar's son in the Bible."

Wow. Keeley's respect meter for Sofia increased. For this woman to take in a child who was the result of an affair was amazing. The hurt must have been unimaginable.

"But, Mom, how have you and Sofia remained such good friends?"

Her mother approached Keeley and knelt in front of her, taking Keeley's hands in hers. "Because she chose to forgive us, like God forgives. I'm sorry I kept this from you. Truly, I am. Can you forgive me?"

Keeley stared into her mother's eyes. Could she? She knew God commanded forgiveness, but right now, she struggled with her mother's betrayal.

"I don't know if I can, Mom. You robbed me of the gift of knowing I had a sister all these years. That's hard to come back from." She yanked her hands away and shot to her feet. "Plus, you've treated me harshly ever since MJ was born. Isn't that hypocritical?"

Keeley bounded from the room, distancing herself from the woman's deception.

If only she could escape out of Olivia Ash's fortified estate as easily.

But her son's protection was more important than her own pain.

Keeley's fan stopped, jerking her awake from a restless sleep. She moaned and peered around her room. Darkness extinguished the normal red light on her computer charging station. What had caused the power to go out? She listened for any storms in the area, but silence greeted her. She realized her mother's generator would kick in, so she closed her eyes, exhaustion sending her back into dream world.

"Now!" a whispered voice said.

Was she dreaming again?

She fluttered her eyes open and found a masked man leaning forward with a pillow in his hands, ready to smother her. A Diglo brother had come for revenge.

Keeley's heartbeat exploded, sending horror throughout her body. How could she fight in her still-weakened state? *Please, Lord.* She mustered strength and pushed her hands upward to block the killer. "No! Help!" She tugged upward on his mask, exposing a barbed-wire choker tattoo on his neck. She thrashed on the bed to free herself from the hunter's grip and extended her hand to hit the panic button her mother had installed.

"Don't bother. We's disabled all security. Your bodyguards ain't coming. My brother is killing your beloved paramedic right now. You both have to pay for Eddie's death." He placed one knee on her shoulder as he stood at the side of her bed, pinning her down. "Then we'll eliminate your mother and take your boy. Mama wants him. He'll love growing up with us boys. We'll teach him to hunt. Kill." He inched closer with the pillow. "G'night, Dr. Ash."

No! Lord, help me fight this brother. Protect MJ, Brett and Mom!

Adrenaline fueled Keeley's feeble body, and she brought both knees upward, knocking her attacker off balance. She grabbed a wad of his hair as he stumbled backward, muttering a spew of curses.

She rolled off the opposite side of the bed and knocked the light in the process, crashing it on the hardwood floor. Keeley had to make noise. Surely, Terry and Vic would hear the ruckus and come.

She swallowed to clear her parched throat. "Help! Help!"

"Davey, abort," a hushed voice said through the hunter's radio. "Paramedic slugged me, but I got away."

"Keeley!" Pounding footfalls followed Brett's cry.

Relief washed over Keeley's tensed shoulders. *Brett is safe.*

"Dimwits. Do I have to do everything?" another voice barked. "Get back here. Now that we know how to get around their defenses, we'll attack again."

The brother dashed out of Keeley's room, knocking into Brett in the process.

Brett regained his footing and flew over to Keeley, bringing her into his arms. "Are you okay?"

Words caught in Keeley's throat.

A shotgun blast echoed throughout the house.

Keeley pushed out of Brett's hold, still clasping the wad of hair she'd torn from her attacker. "MJ!"

They raced out of her room into the shadowy hallway.

Keeley tripped over something blocking the corridor. She grasped Brett's arm, breaking her fall. She returned her focus to the object in question. Dim lighting from the kitchen shone a thin beam onto the floor.

Vic lay motionless, crimson spreading on his white shirt.

"No!" Keeley buried her face in Brett's chest.

The Diglos had gotten dangerously close to their family. Again.

THIRTEEN

Brett rubbed his neck where his assailant had gripped after Brett knocked the pillow from his hands. He guessed it would soon show redness and bruises. Thankfully, Brett had been able to punch the brother, then kicked him away before the man fled out of the room. Brett had regained his breath and headed to Keeley's room just as her attacker escaped.

Keeley and Brett had checked on MJ only to find him still fast asleep—even with all the noise.

Thank You, God, for that gift.

Keeley had placed the brother's hair in a plastic bag to give to the constables.

Olivia had come running soon after Brett and Keeley had discovered Vic's body. However, only the shotgun blast woke Terry. He'd claimed to be a deep sleeper and stressed that he wasn't supposed to be on duty anyway. He hadn't heard anything else. Odd. Wouldn't a bodyguard be more alert to his surroundings?

The group now all sat around the dining room table, waiting for Constables Jackson and Antoine to return from their perimeter sweep. The duo responded to Brett's 911 call, along with paramedics. After ensuring everyone was okay, Tina and Otto left while the constables continued their search for the brothers on the property.

Olivia fixated her eyes on something across the room as she fiddled with a place mat on the table. Clearly, the attack had left the normally authoritative judge on edge, but who could blame her? Her fortress had crumbled at the hands of the brother army. Somehow.

Brett observed Terry's expression. The man sat with his weapon resting on his knee, void of expression. Why hadn't Vic's death affected him emotionally? Yes, the tough body-guard rarely revealed his feelings, but seeing Vic's lifeless eyes should have caused some type of reaction. But no emotion passed over the man's face.

Suspicion spiraled around Brett's spine like a corkscrew. Could he have helped the Diglo brothers enter the home? Had he turned off the power? If not, how did they get through the gate? Multiple questions filled Brett's mind, but one thing rose to the top.

They weren't safe in Olivia Ash's home any longer.

The brothers knew where she lived and how to bypass her security.

Steps pounded in the hallway.

Terry sprang to his feet, weapon raised.

The constables entered and stopped.

Jackson raised his hands. "Whoa, put it down, Terry. It's only us."

The man obeyed. "You should have knocked. Good way to get yourselves killed."

Antoine moved closer to the bodyguard. "You have a permit for that?"

"Of course. I'm a professional." Terry holstered the Glock and took his seat. "What did you find? How did these men get by our defenses?"

Jackson pulled out a chair and sat beside Brett. "You tell us. We couldn't find any trace of cut wires. Someone messed with the fuse box, which knocked out the power."

Questions filled Brett's mind. "But wouldn't that have cut the security?"

Olivia's eyes snapped back to the group. "I have state-of-the-art security. Only a code can disarm it, and I've been changing it daily the last few days."

"Well, someone leaked the code." Antoine took a notebook from his vest pocket. "Who has access to it?"

"Myself, Keeley, Terry and…" Her sentence trailed off.

"Vic." Keeley reached for her mother's hand but pulled back.

Brett knew the mother and daughter had exchanged words after Keeley discovered Zoe was her half sister—a secret her mother had kept. Their strained relationship deepened, and the two had barely spoken at the dinner table or looked at each other.

He massaged his tense neck muscles before checking the time. Two in the morning. No wonder Brett was exhausted. The lack of sleep and fighting off an assailant had depleted his energy.

"So, someone in this room gave them the code." Jackson extracted his notebook and scribbled on it.

Terry slammed his hand on the table. "I would not do that."

Jackson focused on Terry. "Not even for a price?"

The bodyguard flew to his feet, knocking his chair onto the floor.

The noise echoed.

"Quiet!" Keeley's whispered command spoke volumes. "You're gonna wake MJ. I don't want him knowing what happened."

Olivia threw up her hands. "Everyone, calm down. This is my house, and I won't tolerate unfounded accusations." The judge had reverted back into her authoritative mode.

The case that had ended Brett's policing career entered his mind. "There's another possibility. They hacked your system remotely and disarmed your security that way." That was how the black-hat hacker had entered their secured premises where Brett was guarding a witness.

"That has to be it. I trust my bodyguards and Keeley explicitly." Her eyes glared at Jackson. "They wouldn't betray me. They know better than to cross a judge."

Keeley toyed with the strings on her sweatshirt. "Is there some way to check if someone got into the system?"

"We'll get Digital Forensics to look into it." Jackson addressed Brett and Keeley. "Can either of you tell me anything about your attackers? What they looked like? Did they say anything? That sort of thing."

"Mine wore a mask and full hunting gear," Brett said. "When I fought him off, he swore and ran."

Keeley raised her index finger. "Wait. My attacker said we had to pay for killing Eddie. I'm guessing that was the younger brother. Then another called my attacker Davey. Back when we stopped to help those fugitives, they mentioned the name Eddie, too, and someone named Roy."

Jackson scribbled in his notebook. "So, a Davey, a Roy and an Eddie. I'm guessing their real name isn't Diglo. However, that's more than what we had." He flipped a page. "I should also tell you we found the knife they used to stab Spokene and Hopkins. We're checking it now, but I doubt we'll find prints on it."

"Wait!" Brett went to the counter and picked up the plastic bag. "Keeley was smart enough to pull out some hair. Perhaps you can get DNA from this." He handed it to Jackson.

The constable smiled. "Good work. I'll take it to Ginger." He placed it in his vest pocket. "Anything else?"

Keeley twirled a curl before her sad eyes brightened. "Oh, I almost forgot. I caught a glimpse of a strange tattoo on his neck."

"Can you describe it, Keeley?" Jackson poised his pen.

"It appeared to be barbed-wire links, but they weren't joined and looked like a choker."

"We'll check with local tattoo artists." Jackson jotted down a note in his book.

Brett rubbed his neck again, warding off the pain still lingering from the brother's tight grip. "Hopefully you'll get a break with that information. Can you keep us updated? With what you can, of course."

"I will. There's a lot at stake here." Jackson's expression softened. "I hate to tell you all this, but we're gonna need you to vacate the premises. This is now a crime scene, and they have to do a thorough investigation inside and out of your property."

Olivia burst upright. "What? I refuse to leave my home."

Keeley latched on to her hand, tugging her back into the chair. "Mom, you have to."

"I recommend you separate as well." Antoine tapped his pen on the table. "Judge Ash, do you have someone you could stay with? Take Terry."

Her jaw dropped as her gaze traveled to Keeley. "I can't leave my daughter and grandson."

"Constables and Terry, could you leave the room for a minute? I need to talk to my mother and Brett alone."

Jackson looked at Keeley as he stood. "Of course. We'll be in the living room calling our forensics team."

The trio left.

Keeley took her mother's hands in hers. "Mom, I know you don't want to hear this, but I think separating is a good idea."

"Well, then perhaps Brett could go back to his father's!"

"I'm not leaving Keeley and my son." Brett tightened his jaw.

Keeley eyed him, a smile tugging at her lips. "You believe me now?"

"I do."

Keeley turned back to Olivia. "Maybe you could stay with the Coates family. The mayor can add more security."

Olivia's eyes narrowed. "Are you punishing me because I didn't tell you about Zoe?"

"Not punishing, just distancing myself. I'm sorry, but I need a break from you right now." She expelled a long breath. "It will be good for us. Don't worry. We'll keep in touch—for MJ's sake."

"I don't like it." Olivia's words spewed anger.

"Mom, you, of all people, should know there are consequences to our actions."

The woman leaned back in the chair, folding her arms.

Brett squirmed, not knowing how to react to the tension between mother and daughter. However, he needed to break the sudden silence.

A plan formed, and he grazed Keeley's arm. "Keels, we need to get out of Carimoose Bay. It's not safe here any longer. It's obvious the brothers can find us." Brett wasn't sure how she'd take the next news, but he had to be honest. "We need to go into hiding. No one—" he looked at Olivia "—and I mean no one can know where we are. It's for all our sakes."

"Is that really necessary?"

"Trust me. I know I'm not a police officer any longer, but my training is still here." He tapped on his temple.

Olivia placed her hands on the table and rose slowly. "I'm tired of hearing that."

"Mom. Settle down." Keeley's voice conveyed her anger. "We have to find a location the Diglo brothers don't know about. They seem to be able to find us wherever we go, and you're a public figure. They know you're my mother."

Olivia marched out of the room without saying a word.

"Sorry about that. Her ego has been taken down a notch, and she doesn't like it." She rubbed his arm. "I'm so glad you finally believe MJ is yours."

"Me too."

She twirled a curl. "But where should we hide?"

"My father has a cabin just outside Carimoose Bay, deep in the Elimac Forest. As you know, that section of woods extends for miles. We could go there."

She let go of her hair. "Does it have internet and cell reception? I want to stay connected to the case—and Mom."

"It's spotty, but it works. I'm going to talk to Layke. He'll get us supplies for protection. I'll find out what he suggests. Pack quickly."

Keeley stood. "What about your dad? Should we bring him?"

"I can't risk moving him, and I can't leave you alone." Caught between two families. But Brett knew what his father would want.

To protect his only grandson.

Keeley shifted her son in her arms and followed Brett into a rustic cabin three hours later. Layke had agreed to Brett's plan and provided them with two sat phones as well as flashlights. He promised he'd arrange for regular patrols in the cabin's vicinity. He also warned them about telling anyone their whereabouts. Hiding was their highest form of protection. Since they didn't know who they could trust, they had to sever communication with their colleagues and any other friends at this point. Keeley hated that it had come to this but realized its necessity. She sent a vague email to her coworkers explaining she required time off and wouldn't be available. Keeley requested Beth cancel her classes for the next couple of weeks. She didn't want to give Audrey the burden of juggling everything. The students could wait.

Brett had also contacted his partner Tina to let her know he'd be unavailable for the next few days. Brett said she tried to get more information from him and didn't like that he wouldn't tell her.

Keeley hugged her mother before they left her estate and promised to stay in touch. She had kissed her cheek and told her she loved her, despite her indiscretion. Keeley couldn't leave her mother without expressing her love, even if she was still furious with her.

Brett flicked on the light in the cabin, revealing an open kitchen and living area with three bedrooms in the rear. A stone fireplace displayed photos on the mantel.

"I'll turn up the heat and get the groceries from the Jeep."

He adjusted the dial on the wall box. "It's not Olivia's estate, but it's cozy." Brett reached for MJ. "I can put him in the middle bedroom. You take the one on the right."

Keeley handed her son to his father. "I can't sleep. Okay if I sit here for a bit? I need to unwind before trying to go back to bed."

"Sure." He lifted MJ and tipped his chin in the kitchen's direction. "Put on some tea. I'd love one."

"Good idea."

Ten minutes later, Brett returned from tucking MJ into bed and putting the groceries in the fridge.

"Your tea is ready." Keeley sat curled up on the couch with the plaid blanket wrapped around her, sipping her tea. "You were gone longer than I expected."

"I wanted to make sure he didn't wake up and get scared being in a strange place." He grabbed the mug and plunked himself in the rocking chair across from her. "Do you want me to make a fire to help take the chill off?"

"I'm good."

"I'm not sure I believe you. It's been a tough few hours." He grimaced. "Well, longer than that. We've been through a lot in a short period."

"Sure have. We've been targeted multiple times, and I found out I had a half sister I didn't know about." She took another sip of the passionflower tea. "My mother has lied to me all my life."

"I'm so sorry. That must be tough to digest."

"More than tough. She not only kept this secret, but her affair was the catalyst that brought my father's heart attack on."

Brett jolted forward, spilling his tea. "What?"

"Well, not exactly. Apparently my dad had a heart condition they didn't know about. After he discovered Mom's affair with Yannick, his anger put him into cardiac arrest." She bit her lip, fighting the pending tears. "I barely remember my father."

"That must have been hard. Growing up without a father and with a—"

"Domineering mother? Yup. Sure was, and I did everything to please her but never seemed to be able to."

"Why do you think that was? You've become a successful career woman. Shouldn't that account for something?" He drank his tea.

"You'd think, but no. From the time I was a teenager, my mother impressed upon me to become something more than those around me."

"Let me guess. She wanted you to go into law."

"Good guess."

Brett rubbed his finger around the rim of his mug. "How long did she practice law before she became a judge?"

"About twenty years. Becoming a judge is highly competitive, but she knew people and was connected within the Yukon."

"And I'm sure the mayor helped."

"Well, he wasn't the mayor at the time of their affair, but yes, eventually. I watched her through her years in law, and I didn't like the woman she'd become." Keeley set her tea down and inched the blanket closer to her neck. "She worked long hours and barely had time for me. However, she always made time for Zoe." Jealousy over her deceased half sister rose. *Lord, forgive me.*

"Why would she do that?"

"At first I thought it was because she was excited that Sofia finally had a child and she wanted to share in her happiness, but as Zoe grew into a teenager, she expressed an interest in becoming a lawyer. So, of course, Mom loved that. Someone other than her own daughter wanted to walk in her footsteps. The irony of that statement isn't lost on me now." Keeley got up and walked to the mantel, studying the pictures of Brett as a child, his mom and dad, and another young boy. A brother or a childhood friend? He'd never mentioned a sibling.

"So, that angered you?"

She turned and sighed. "I'm ashamed to admit that. Zoe and I were friends, but not close." Her lip quivered. "I regret that now. My mother robbed me of the knowledge of having a sister. I'm not sure I can forgive her."

"I'm sorry. Seems like I'm saying that a lot tonight."

"Not your fault." Keeley stepped to the window and peered into the darkness. Only a single beam of moonlight filtered through the trees. "It's peaceful here. I can see why you chose it. Secluded and out in God's nature. Great combination. How did your father take the news of us leaving?"

"He totally understood and said if I hadn't left, he would have ordered me to."

She smiled at the thought of the sweet older man demanding anything of his son. "How's he doing?"

"Still eating. That's promising, but I know what's coming." He finished his tea and returned to the kitchen. "I hate being apart from him, but I need to look after my family."

His family. Keeley loved the sound of that, but was he still going to take that promotion? Time to change the subject. "Did you come here a lot as a boy?"

Brett smiled. "Yes, whenever we could. Dad was busy on the police force, so we took every opportunity to head here. He called the cabin his oasis from crime."

Keeley walked around the main room, studying the decor. "I can see why. Did your mom come, too? You said she was away a lot."

"She came when she was home from her medical missions." Brett chuckled. "She loved to fry up the fish we caught in the creek. I can almost taste it now. So good."

Keeley returned to the mantel and picked up another photo. Brett stood, raising a fish in one hand as his other rested on the younger boy's shoulder. She tapped on the boy's face. "Who's this?"

Brett's eyes saddened. "My brother, Gideon."

"I didn't realize you had a brother. Where is he?"

Pain contorted Brett's handsome face. "He passed years ago." Brett held his mug over the sink.

"I'm so sorry. How did he die?"

Brett fumbled with his mug, and it slipped from his fingers, crashing to the floor.

Keeley hurried to his side and squatted, picking up the shattered pieces.

"I'd rather not talk about Gideon. I'm heading to bed." He left the room, not bothering to help her with his mess.

What just happened? What about his brother's death haunted Brett?

Something told her it wasn't good.

FOURTEEN

Brett slipped out of his bed and tiptoed into the kitchen. The hour was still early, and sleep evaded him. He had tossed and turned but couldn't settle after such a horrifying experience. Images of his attacker and his conversation with Keeley flooded his head, keeping his overactive mind from shutting off. He prayed Keeley had been able to rest.

The broom leaning against the wall reminded Brett of his clumsy accident, and he grimaced. Why had he reacted the way he did last night? His brother had been gone for years, but her question about Gideon's death had transported him back to that terrifying day. The day he left his little brother alone in the house. Why didn't he share it with Keeley instead of making a fool of himself? *You know why.*

He still carried the guilt over his brother's death. His shame subconsciously made him stuff the memories of that day into a box and slam the lid shut. Her question brought it all tumbling back.

Sometimes God allows us to enter the wilderness to shape us. Mold us.

His father's earlier words drifted into Brett's mind. Was he correct? *Does God take us into the wilderness to shape us?*

Let Him in.

Could he do as his father said and surrender to God?

Brett ignored his silent question and took coffee from a cupboard. Since he couldn't sleep, he required caffeine to give him a kick start to the day. He wanted to take MJ to Brett's favorite fishing spot and show him all the places he'd loved as a kid.

Excitement fueled his energy. *I still can't believe I have a son.*

One positive thing in his otherwise-messed-up world.

Brett filled the water reservoir, added the grinds to the basket and hit the power button.

Shuffling footsteps sounded behind him, and he whirled around.

Keeley wiped her eyes and dropped into a chair at the kitchen table. "Good—you're making coffee. I could use a huge cup."

"Didn't sleep?"

She shook her head. "Not much. Not that the bed wasn't comfortable, just not my own."

"I understand." Brett opened the fridge door. "Bacon and eggs for breakfast?"

"Sounds great. I'm shocked MJ didn't wake up screaming. He can be unsettled in new places."

Brett withdrew the food and set it on the countertop. "Well, this cabin is peaceful, so maybe that helped."

The coffee maker crackled as the liquid dripped into the carafe, wafting a delightful aroma into the room.

"Can I help?"

"No, you stay there." Brett eyed the broom. "Listen, I'm sorry about last night. I owe you an explanation."

She raised her hands. "No, it's okay. You don't. I shouldn't have pried."

"Gideon died at the age of twelve, and it was my fault." Brett lifted a frying pan from a wall hook.

Keeley's jaw dropped. "I somehow doubt it's your fault. Tell me what happened." She fiddled with her housecoat belt. "Only if you want to."

"I was fifteen and had some friends over, playing video games. Mom was on one of her trips, and Dad was on shift." Brett added bacon to the pan and turned on the burner. "Gideon kept interrupting us and I got annoyed, so we went to the local park and shot some hoops. I told him not to come. He was twelve and old enough to stay alone."

Keeley placed her hand on his back. "What happened?"

He startled as he failed to hear her approach. He turned.

Her softened eyes revealed her concern. "Tell me."

"A member of one gang Dad put away threw Molotov cocktails into the window. The place caught fire, and my brother died." He rubbed his heavy chest as if that would relieve his guilt. "I can't forgive myself for leaving him alone."

She caressed his arm. "You didn't cause the fire. It's not your fault, Brett."

"My father said the same thing. Why can't I put it behind me?" He added another frying pan to the stove. "Your mother robbed you of knowing you had a sister. I robbed myself of my brother."

"Don't do that to yourself. You need to let it go. Stop beating—"

"Mama!" MJ screamed from the bedroom.

"Oh dear. He woke up and doesn't know where we are. I'll be back." Keeley headed to the bedroom and, moments later, reemerged with MJ in tow. "See, we're at Mr. Brett's cabin. Isn't this a neat place?"

Brett smiled at his son's open mouth as the boy studied the rustic setting.

"Cool." He ran to a cabinet near the window and pointed. "What's in here?"

Brett turned off the burner and moved to where MJ stood. "That's our game cabinet." He opened the front doors. "Check it out."

Multiple board games, movies and books lined the shelves. Gideon used to refer to it as their toy cabinet. Once again, sadness washed over Brett, but he suppressed the sudden memories of his brother. He had to focus on getting to know his son.

MJ's eyes widened, and he brought out a checkerboard, placing it on the table. "I love checkers. Can we play?"

Brett chuckled. Gideon and Brett had spent hours playing the game when they were younger. "Of course, but how about some breakfast first?"

MJ bounced on his tippy-toes. "Yes!"

Keeley held her hand out. "Let's go wash up, slugger."

Two and a half hours later, after breakfast, a game of checkers, and a hike to the lake and back, MJ sat in front of the television watching cartoons.

Brett had reached out to Nancy using one of the sat phones. She reported no change in his father's condition.

Keeley nursed another cup of coffee as she viewed her emails. Thankfully the internet was working today. For now. It kicked in and out at his father's cabin.

Keeley took a sip and set her mug down. "Oh my. Come and look at this picture Layke sent."

Brett positioned himself behind her chair and leaned over her shoulder.

A photo of an unlinked barbed-wire tattoo was displayed on her screen.

She pointed. "This is the same one as my attacker's."

"Does Layke say anything else? Did they identify who the tattoo belongs to?"

"He said he'd call—"

The sat phone rang in Brett's hand. "That's gotta be him." He pressed the appropriate buttons and used the hands-free option. "Brett here."

"It's Layke. Did you guys get the picture?"

"Yes, we're looking at it now. You found this fast. What can you tell us about it?"

"Constable Antoine visited a few shops and got a hit. We found the tattoo artist. He operates a shady business and doesn't keep records, but he remembers the man. Said his name was

Davey, and he bragged about getting a big score, so he thought the tattoo would make him look tough."

"Davey was my attacker. It has to be the same person. When did he say this?"

"Says he was in approximately fourteen months ago."

Keeley's gaze popped to Brett's, her eyes widening. "Wait—isn't that around the same time the hikers went missing? Could there be a connection?"

"Possibly. But I have something else."

Brett held his breath in anticipation of the constable's news.

"No prints on the knife, but it was definitely the one used to kill Cameron and stab Hopkins. The coroner confirmed that the unique markings on Cameron's body matched the blade. Hopkins is recovering nicely but said he didn't see his attacker because the perp surprised him from behind. He remembers seeing two hunters before he passed out." Shuffling papers sounded over the phone. "However, we got DNA from the hair, and we're checking all databases to see if there's a match. That might take a while."

Brett whistled. "That was quick."

"Yeah, the mayor has put the pressure on us to find his daughter's killer. Not that I blame him," Jackson said. "Just wanted to keep you apprised. I'm praying this is a step in solving both the cold case and the attacks on you."

"I hope so." Brett checked to ensure MJ hadn't been listening.

His eyes were still fixated on the television. Good.

A thought entered Brett's mind. "Wait, Keels. I just remembered something you said back at the Diglos' cabin. You said Eddie looked familiar. Do you remember from where?"

She snapped her fingers. "I forgot about that." She twisted a chunk of her red hair as if that would help her thinking process. "No, I can't remember. So frustrating."

Brett placed his hand on her shoulder. "It's okay. It will come to you."

She huffed. "Hopefully."

"If it does, contact me right away. We have cruisers patrolling your area around the clock. I'll let you know if we spot anything suspicious. We're in close contact with each officer out there." The constable cleared his throat. "I'm praying for you both. God's got you."

Brett bristled. Could he believe that when a malicious gang was out there targeting his family?

Keeley studied Brett's pained face as he paced the living room area after the constable's call. Was it talk of the Diglo brothers that worried Brett or the fact that Layke had mentioned God? *Lord, I sense a battle raging in Brett's heart. Can You calm his doubts and show him You're there? He needs You. I need You, too. Father, I'm struggling on why we're going through this hardship. I—*

A ding on her laptop halted her prayers. She clicked her email program and found a message from Beth requesting Keeley call her right away at the lab. It was important.

"I gotta make a call." Not trusting her cell phone's reception, Keeley snatched the sat and punched in the lab's number.

"Beth Bower speaking."

"Beth, it's Keeley." Keeley walked to the window and peered at the sky. Dark clouds had moved in again. Great. That was all they needed. A storm in the middle of nowhere.

"Oh, hey. I wasn't sure it was you, as the number's blocked. Where are you calling from?"

Beth's question jolted Keeley back to her conversation. "Sat phone. Poor reception here. What's going on?"

"Just got a call from someone looking for you."

Why did that warrant the urgent message to call? People telephoned her lab all the time. "Who was it?"

"Someone named Davey. Said he was a good friend of yours who needed to get in touch with you right away. He wanted to know where to reach you."

Keeley caught Brett's attention. "What did you tell him?"

Brett raised a brow.

"That I didn't know, because I don't. I wouldn't have told him anyway. I realize there are creeps after you, and this guy sounded—I don't know—antsy." A pause. "I was scared it was one of those Diglo brothers."

Wait. Keeley tensed. She'd never mentioned the Diglo brothers to Beth. Had she? Suspicion turned Keeley's breakfast into lead. First Audrey and now Beth. Did she know her coworkers as well as she thought? Was Beth feeding them information all this time, and this was a ruse to give up their location?

"Did you hear me, boss?"

Keeley gripped the phone tighter. "Sorry, what did you ask?"

"Can you tell me where you are? I just need to know you're safe."

No one can know where we are.

Brett's words filtered through Keeley's mind. At this point, she didn't know who to trust. Not even her assistant. "I can't tell you, but I'm safe."

"But what if I need to get in touch with you? In case this Davey calls again?"

Keeley massaged her lower back. "Email me. Is there anything else?"

"I wish you'd tell me." Her voice faltered.

"Beth, I can't." How much clearer did she have to get?

"Fine. Be that way." *Click.*

Wow. What had warranted Beth's shift in disposition? She normally was a fun-loving woman.

"What was that all about?"

Keeley set the phone on the table. "Beth telling me Davey called looking for me, but she acted strangely."

"In what way?"

"Well, she mentioned the Diglo brothers, and I'm pretty sure I never gave her their name. Plus, she got mad at me when

I wouldn't tell her where I was." Keeley rubbed her left palm with her right thumb. "She's never gotten upset with me before. Something isn't right."

"Let's not jump to conclusions. Beth was probably having a bad day and missing you. But we should mention it to Layke. Just in case." Brett raised his index finger. "Wait—that reminds me. Tina acted strange the other day, too."

Keeley twirled her hair, then dropped it as if it had scorched her fingers. "Do you think the leader of this group could be someone close to us?"

"Right now, I don't trust anyone. Perhaps Layke can do a deep dive into all of their backgrounds."

Keeley bit her lip. She hated spying on friends. "Sure." A tear formed and fell before she could stop it.

Brett flew to her side, bringing her into a hug. "It's gonna be okay."

She melted into his arms. *I want to stay here forever. It feels like home.* "I just want all of this to be over."

"I understand. Me too." He squeezed tighter.

"Hug time!" MJ plowed into their legs and wrapped his little arms around them. "Mr. Brett, I love you."

Brett stiffened in her arms.

Keeley pulled back from his embrace and stared into his eyes, asking him a silent question on her mind. *Are you staying?*

He looked away, but not before she caught his wrenched expression.

He *was* leaving.

Keeley dug her fingernails into her palms, curbing her frustration. She couldn't let MJ see her disappointment.

Brett tousled MJ's curls. "You too. How about some lunch, sport?"

"Yes. Then more checkers?" MJ clapped.

Brett folded his arms, tapping his index finger on his upper arm. "You just want to beat me again, don't you?"

MJ giggled.

Keeley suppressed a sigh and returned to her laptop. *He can't commit, so close that crack in your heart you let open up.*

Had she misread him? She thought they were getting closer and their spark had reignited.

How could I have been so wrong?

Keeley wiggled her mouse to bring her laptop back to life.

She sucked in an audible ragged breath.

Her black screen held a message in bold red letters.

We will find you. You can't hide forever.

Had Beth sent this message? The timing couldn't be a co-incidence.

Or had the Diglos hacked her computer?

FIFTEEN

Brett snapped a picture of Keeley's screen seconds before it pixelated and changed to a skull and crossbones, then disappeared. His pulse elevated. This proved someone connected to the Diglos had serious hacking skills. Or it was one of the brothers. Brett quickly tapped on his cell phone, sending the picture and details to Constable Jackson.

Keeley stumbled backward, gasping for breath. "Can't breathe."

"Mama?" MJ ran to his mother's side, his eyes widening with each of Keeley's sharp intakes.

She was hyperventilating.

Brett darted to the kitchen and snatched a paper grocery bag. "Keels, breathe into this." He scrunched the top to create a small passageway and handed it to her. "Slow, deep breaths."

He yanked out a chair. "Sit."

She sat and lifted it to her mouth, breathing in. Out. In. Out. After a minute, her rhythm slowed, and she removed the bag from her mouth. "Thanks."

MJ tugged at her arm. "Mama, you okay?"

"I'm good, slugger. Sorry for scaring you. Go grab a book, and we'll read before lunch."

He smiled and skipped to the toy cabinet.

"Thanks, Brett." Keeley set the bag on the table.

"Do you hyperventilate often?"

"Not normally, and I almost did in the forest when the brothers attacked. But this time they got into my computer, and it shocked me. They're getting closer." She inhaled another deep breath.

Brett sat. He must calm her. Her pale face told him she still struggled. He rubbed her arm. "It's gonna be okay." He glanced at her laptop. Something niggled at the back of his brain. "Keels, do you really think the Diglo brothers are capable of hacking systems?"

She shook her head. "Honestly? No."

"Why do you say that?"

"Just a hunch. Their odd dialect makes me feel like they may not have finished school." She held her hands out, palms up. "Not judging or anything, but they just don't seem the computer types."

"Who could be the hacker, then? This Mama they referred to?"

"Possibly."

MJ squealed and shot to his mother's side, interrupting their conversation. "Can we read this one?"

"Good choice, slugger." Keeley got up and nudged him toward the couch.

"I'll start lunch." Brett watched the two snuggle together, and a picture formed in his mind.

The three of them sitting together with MJ in the center as they read a book in front of a Christmas tree.

Would that happen?

Could he trust that the woman before him wouldn't betray him like all the others?

She'd certainly never given him any sign of that, but she'd pulled away from him more than once lately. Just when he thought they were getting closer.

She doesn't want you around, Brett.

And that broke his heart.

Later that night, MJ yawned as the coals in the fireplace held his focus. Brett had wanted to keep them toasty, so he had built a fire earlier. They had taken a walk in the afternoon, staying close to the cabin. MJ had made Brett promise to take him fishing sometime soon.

If only.

"I think it's bedtime," Brett whispered.

"Agree." Keeley uncurled her legs and moved to get up.

Brett eased her back down. "Let me do it. How about you make us some tea? I promise not to break my mug this time." He smiled and scooped up MJ, taking him into the bedroom.

He placed him on the bed, covering him with the quilted bear-and-moose comforter. Brett tucked it in all around MJ's little body—something his father used to do with Brett and Gideon. He'd said they were snug as a bug and could sleep better.

Brett smiled at the memory and kissed MJ's forehead. "Night, my sweet son," he whispered.

He squared his shoulders. Time to ask Keeley the question he'd been waiting to ask. First a tea to calm them both. Brett slipped out of the room, easing the door shut. He walked to the kitchen, where she'd been boiling water. Brett placed a lavender tea bag in a mug. "Are you feeling better?"

She poured the water into both cups. "Much, thanks. I just want to relax for a bit before turning in. Hoping for a better sleep tonight."

"Sounds good."

They took their teas and sat together on the couch.

Brett fished out his cell phone from his back pocket and placed it on the log coffee table in front of them.

"Brett, I've been wondering something." Keeley paused. "Why did you leave policing? Wasn't that your passion?"

He slumped against the couch. Could he own up to the mistake he'd made? If he wanted her to trust him, he had to give something in return. Right?

Brett took a sip of his tea as if that would give him courage. "It was once. Until a mistake I made cost my partner's life."

Her mouth dropped. "What?"

He shut his eyes, trying to erase the picture in his head from that day. The picture etched in his mind. *Time to face the past, Brett.*

Brett opened his eyes. "My partner and I, along with other constables, were tasked with protecting a key witness in a huge case, so we were patrolling outside the safe house. The witness had gone to bed, and the place was secured. We were rechecking the perimeter when we heard an explosion." He clenched his jaw. "We rushed around to the back only to find our cruiser in flames. We had hidden it behind the house on a side street to conceal our presence."

"Oh no. What happened?"

Brett set his cup down and got up, moving to the window. He brushed the drapes aside and checked to ensure they were still alone. *Humph. Old habits.* He turned back to face Keeley. "We called it in, but the perp used it as a diversion and hacked into the system. They somehow gained entry using the code. The witness screamed, and we ran inside." The scene flashed again.

Blood. So much blood.

"There were two of them. One stood in between the bodies of our constable and the witness. He turned his gun on me, and I dodged behind a counter. The other perp caught my partner by surprise and held her at knifepoint. Said we had to pay for interfering. He stabbed her before I could even react. Then the pair fled." Brett bit his lip to ward off pending tears. "I didn't save her."

He slumped back onto the couch and held his head in his hands.

Keeley wrapped her arm around him. "But, Brett, how can you say you made a mistake?"

He lifted his head. "Because I didn't properly enter the house. I should have seen the second man."

"It's still not your fault." She rubbed his back. "So that's why you switched to becoming a paramedic?"

"Yes. I didn't have the right tools to save her and never

wanted to be in that situation again." He grimaced. "I hated to tell my cop father, but he took it well. Said he was proud of me."

"You're an amazing man, Brett Ryerson, and don't you forget that."

"Thank you. I decided when I came back to the Yukon to also train with Search and Rescue. I looked into it, and they were happy about the possibility because they wanted to add a paramedic to their team."

"That's awesome. Seems we're both furthering ourselves. I've been taking a self-defense class."

What? "Why? Did something happen?"

"No. Just wanted a break from single parenting and work for one night a week."

"Good idea." He gazed into her beautiful hazel eyes. *I could get lost there.* "Keels, can I ask you a question?"

"Sure."

"Can we tell MJ I'm his dad now?"

His cell phone buzzed, and a message appeared on the screen.

Need your decision. Are you coming back?

Brett noted Keeley's hardened eyes. She'd seen the text.

"You're leaving, aren't you?" The disdain in her voice revealed her disappointment.

He didn't want to. *Ask me to stay.* He gnawed on his lower lip. "No, I'm not."

She bolted upright. "You hesitated. Not sure I believe you. So, until you're sure, we don't tell MJ." She scrambled out of the room, slamming her bedroom door behind her.

Once again, Brett buried his head in his hands.

Convince her you're staying.

Keeley woke to laughing coming from the living room. She groaned and checked her smartwatch: 8:00 a.m. She popped into an upright seated position. How had she slept that long?

Then she remembered… She'd had a hard time getting to sleep after seeing the text from Brett's leader in Ontario. His response to her question didn't convince her. *He's leaving.*

And her heart was broken.

She had cried herself to sleep. He had worked his way back into her heart so quickly. Not that she was surprised. Their previous connection had been strong.

MJ's giggle coming from the living room stuck in the imaginary knife, deepening her wound.

Oh, Brett, how could you?

Keeley had watched her son get closer and closer to his father without even knowing his true identity.

A squeal sounded, followed by thudding steps.

Brett must be chasing MJ.

Keeley fell back onto her pillow and rubbed her eyes, feeling a bulge. *Ugh!* How could she face them with puffy eyes? *They'll know.*

MJ will know.

Preston's face entered her mind, and she sat up.

Get it together, Keeley. You've done this before. You can do it again.

For MJ's sake.

She just wished she didn't have to.

Keeley squared her shoulders and rolled out of bed. *Time to face the music, as they say.*

After dressing in jeans and a green sweatshirt, she proceeded into the hall, tiptoeing into the bathroom. She splashed multiple handfuls of cold water onto her face, hoping to shrink the puffs. However, it didn't help.

So be it.

She inhaled deeply and plastered on a smile before thrusting open the door. "Morning, boys. What's going on out here? All this noise is gonna wake the animals outside."

"No, it won't, Mama. Don't be silly." MJ threw himself into her arms. "You're a sleepyhead."

Keeley stole a peek at Brett, but he had moved into the kitchen and turned his back to her, obviously distancing himself. She kissed her son's head. "Morning, slugger. Did you sleep okay?"

"Yup. Guess what?" He returned to Brett's side.

"What?"

"Mr. Brett is making us pancakes this morning. My favorite."

She laughed. "Everything is your favorite."

"No. I don't like broccoli." He scrunched his nose. "Ewww."

"That's true. You spit it out whenever Gramma tries to hide it in her veggie lasagna." Keeley meandered into the kitchen.

MJ pushed a stool next to the counter and climbed up, sticking his finger in the pancake batter.

Brett play-slapped his hand away. "Hey now. None of that." He met Keeley's gaze. "Trust me. You don't want your mother mad at you."

She ignored the implication and brought out plastic plates from a cupboard. "Slugger, help me set the table."

"Yes, Mama." He hopped down from the stool and extended his arms. "I'm a good helper."

"You are. Now hold tight." Keeley set the plates in his hands.

He trudged toward the dining area, taking baby steps. "What are we doing today? Can we go fishing, Mr. Brett?"

"We can if it's okay with your mom. It's supposed to be warmer."

After a day of catering to MJ's every whim, Keeley tucked her son into bed. They said their nightly prayers, and she kissed his forehead. "Sleep well."

"I will, Mama. I had fun with Mr. Brett today. Can you marry him so he can live with us forever?"

Keeley recoiled as if her son had punched her in the stomach. How could she tell him Brett was leaving?

She pushed a red curl from his eyes. "I don't think that will happen, but you can be friends with Mr. Brett."

His lip quivered. "I want him to be my dad."

So do I.

Once again, she kissed his forehead. "Time for sleep. Love you."

He rolled over and faced the opposite side without another word.

Like father, like son.

Keeley sighed and opened the door, then startled.

Brett stumbled backward, looking down. "Sorry. I didn't mean to eavesdrop. Listen, I need to tell you—"

The sat phone rang, ending their awkward conversation.

One Keeley didn't need right now.

Brett scooped up the phone. "Brett here." A pause. "I'll put you on speaker." He turned to Keeley. "Layke has news."

She nodded and sat.

"Go ahead, Layke."

"Okay, we got a hit off the DNA from the hair. Davey Hawkins. He was in the foster care system. We found a picture of him as a boy and had Scarlet, a renowned forensic artist, do an age progression sketch. She lives in British Columbia now, but she's good—and fast. Sending it to your cell phones. Hopefully you have good reception."

Keeley fished out her cell phone just as it dinged. "Got it." She stared at Davey's evil eyes, a shiver paralyzing her muscles. Scarlet even included the tattoo Keeley had described. Impressive.

Brett whistled. "You said he was in the foster care system. What family?"

"We're still checking into that, as it appears he bounced around for a few years."

Brett tapped his thumb on the table. "So, his last name is Hawkins. Does he have any priors?"

"That's the odd part," Layke said. "No records at all. It's like he doesn't exist. What happened at your mother's and the fact they got into your laptop tells us someone connected with the Diglos is a black-hat hacker."

Keeley tensed. "We came to that conclusion as well. I don't think it's any of the Diglos, though. From the time I spent with them, they just don't seem that smart. I realize I sound judgmental. I don't mean it that way. Just an impression I got." She told him her concerns about Beth.

"Brett mentioned her, and I did a deep dive. That's another bit of news I have. Did you know the police arrested her in her early twenties for assaulting her college roommate?"

Keeley shot upright. "What? How did she get that by me? I did a thorough reference check."

"She was never officially charged. The female dropped her claim. Said she lied."

Keeley strode to the window, twirling her hair. She scanned the area. They still had daylight later in the evenings during this time of year in the Yukon.

"Wait. Antoine is giving me an update." A muffled conversation filtered through the sat phone.

The wrinkles on Brett's forehead revealed his worry.

"Guys, Davey was just spotted near your location."

Brett charged out of his chair. "Where, Layke?"

"About five kilometers. We're sending units to check it out. Stay indoors and alert. I'll reach out when I get further updates." He clicked off.

"Keels, get away from the window." Brett raced to a tall locked cabinet and pressed in a code. He opened the door, revealing a gun collection.

Keeley closed the window drapes and hustled to the center of the room. "What are you doing?"

"Arming myself for the possibility of an intruder." He lifted out a rifle and loaded it. "I need to protect my family."

Keeley sucked in a breath.

The Diglo brothers had found them again. The question was—how?

SIXTEEN

Brett's pulse thundered in his ears, elevating his guard to keep his family safe. And Keeley and MJ were his family. Even if she didn't want him there. She had distanced herself ever since he got the text from his supervisor. He was about to convince her he wasn't taking the job when Constable Jackson called. Right now, he had to secure the perimeter. He wouldn't let past mistakes cloud his judgment.

Brett removed a Glock from the cabinet and passed it to her. "Keels, do you know how to use one of these?"

Her expression contorted. "I've taken lessons. What are you going to do?"

"I need to make sure there's no one out there." He gathered his jacket from the hook and put it on, securing the rifle over his shoulder.

"Layke said to stay inside, Brett." Her shaky words revealed her worry.

He rubbed her arm. "You're safe. I just have to make sure Davey isn't out there." He moved to the entrance. "I'll only be gone five minutes. Bolt the door after I leave and don't let anyone in other than myself or the constables."

She nodded, biting her lip.

Lord, hear me. Please protect Keels and my son.

Brett stepped onto the veranda, senses on high alert.

The lock clicked into place behind him. *Good girl, Keels.*

He raised the rifle and inspected the forest around the

cabin. Five minutes later, he knocked on the cabin door. "Keels, it's me."

She unlocked and opened the door.

He bounded inside and locked them in. "No suspicious sightings. All okay here?"

"Yes." Keeley handed the Glock to him. "Can we lock these back up? I don't want them out with MJ here."

Brett took the weapons and went to the cabinet, entering the code. He tucked the guns away. "Keels, the code is 02161212. My birth date and Gideon's. If you need to get back into the cabinet in case something happens to me."

She threw her arms around him. "Don't say that. Nothing is going to happen to you."

He held her tightly, chin resting on the top of her head. *She fits perfectly in my arms.*

They stayed in the same position for a few minutes. Then he leaned back. Their gazes locked, and his eyes shifted to her lips.

He inched closer, wanting to press his lips on hers.

She tilted her chin upward.

Did she want him to kiss her?

He caressed her cheek and—

The sat phone shrilled, severing the moment.

He broke their embrace and snatched the phone from its docking station. "Brett here."

"We got him," Layke said. "Taking him inside the station now."

Brett turned to Keeley. "They got him." He pressed the speaker button. "You mean Davey?"

"Yes. He was lurking at a store down the road from your location. There are still two brothers at large, so stay put. I left a constable near the entrance to the cabin." A slamming door sounded through the phone.

"Can we listen in? I just want to be sure it's him. I'll recognize his voice." Keeley's twisted expression revealed her apprehension.

"That's not normal, but okay. Keep the line open and wait a sec. We're going to see what we can get out of him. Moving him into an interrogation room now. We won't tell him you're on the line."

Brett pulled out a chair at the table. "Keels, sit," he whispered.

She obeyed.

He sat beside her and placed the phone in the middle of them. Brett motioned for Keeley to remain silent.

A minute later, voices sailed through the phone. Jackson telling the brother to sit, followed by the sound of handcuffs clicking in place.

"Okay, let's begin," Jackson said. "We know you're Davey Hawkins. Tell us what you were doing at that hardware store."

The man swore. "Whatcha think? Shoppin'. You had no right to arrest me. I wants a lawyer."

"Are you part of the Diglo gang? Where are your brothers?"

"I ain't tellin' you squat." His wicked tone shot through the airwaves.

Keeley gripped the sides of the table.

"Did you attack Dr. Ash in her home?" Jackson asked.

A chair scraping sounded. "I did nothin' of the kind. Did Keeley tattle on me?"

"How did you know her name?"

"I—I— She's…" His stammering proved his nervousness.

Keeley grabbed Brett's arm and mouthed, "It's him."

Brett extracted his cell phone from his pocket and texted Jackson, confirming the voice identification. He prayed it would go through. Thankfully, the reception had been good today.

A pause in the conversation sounded before Brett's phone dinged. Jackson.

Okay. Stay on the line for a minute.

"Tell us about this business you have helping fugitives." Jackson continued the interrogation. "Where is your hideout?"

"Not sure what yous talking about."

"What are the names of your brothers? Is it Diglo? We know the youngest was Eddie. Who's Mama? Roy?" Jackson fired question after question.

"Diglo was our dog." Davey snickered. "You'll never find 'em."

"Mama!" MJ appeared at the entrance.

"Who's there?" Davey asked.

Their son just announced their presence.

"Is that the brat? Keeley, we's comin' for ya. You can't hide forever." Once again, evil bull-rushed through the phone.

MJ whimpered.

Brett hit the button to end the call. He'd forgotten to put them on mute. *Stupid, Brett. Stupid.*

He scurried over to MJ and lifted him. "It's okay, sport. You're okay." He held him tight, praying for protection.

Once again, Brett's cell phone dinged. He returned to the table and examined the text. Nancy.

Your dad doesn't have long. You need to come home. Now!

"No!" Brett sank into a chair with his son in his arms. How had his father's condition changed again so rapidly?

He was dying, and the wicked Diglo brothers were coming for Brett's family.

How could he choose?

Keeley noted Brett's haunted expression, and she followed his line of sight to his phone. She turned it toward her and read the message. Her jaw dropped, and she stood, reaching for MJ. "Let me take him back to bed."

He nodded and handed him to her.

"Let's go, slugger. Everything is okay." Keeley took him

back to his bed, tucking him in tightly. "There. You're all nice and snuggly."

"Was that the bad man, Mama?"

She brushed his bangs to the side. "You never mind about him. You're safe here." *Lord, make it so.*

"Will you sing to me, Mama?"

"What song?" She smiled. Leave it to her son to lighten the load.

"'Jesus Loves Me.'"

Keeley cleared her throat and sang her son's favorite song. He was asleep before she finished.

She kissed his forehead before backing out of the room.

"You have a lovely voice."

She jumped. "You scared me." Heat flushed her cheeks. "Thanks. I'm so sorry to hear about your father. What are you going to do?"

His jaw tightened. "I can't leave you and MJ."

She took his hands in hers. "You'll regret not saying good-bye. Get the patrolling constable to park in the cabin's driveway. Just in case." She pointed to the gun cabinet. "I know the code, remember, so I can arm myself."

Brett bit his lip, revealing the trepidation she guessed plagued his body.

Lord, give him strength. "Brett, you have to go."

He snatched the second sat phone. "Okay, I'll call Layke and take this phone with me. Each number is programmed into the other. I want to be able to reach you at all times."

"Understood."

A wave of worry locked every muscle in her body, but she refused to show him. Or he'd never leave.

She wouldn't let that happen. He'd regret not being with his father as he passed.

Keeley studied him as he spoke to Layke, requesting a constable at the cabin.

Brett paced as he raked his hand through his hair. A habit she remembered from years ago.

He stopped at the window, peeking out. "Okay, thanks." He clicked off and turned. "Constable Antoine is on his way."

Keeley picked up Brett's jacket and handed it to him. "Go. Before it's too late."

He blanketed her in his arms. "I have to tell you something."

She pulled back. "What?"

"I'm not taking the job. I'm staying in the Yukon with you and MJ."

Keeley inhaled a sharp breath. "When did you make that decision?"

"As soon as I realized MJ was my son, I knew I couldn't leave. I just haven't been able to tell my former supervisor." A smile danced on his lips. "We've been a tad busy."

He's staying. However, a question remained lodged in Keeley's mind. Did he want a relationship with *her*? Preston had made promises, too. Promises he broke.

Plus, Brett wasn't a believer.

She retreated.

Sadness wrenched his handsome face.

She'd disappointed him again.

A pounding knock sounded.

"Guys, it's me. Constable Antoine. Let me in."

Brett grabbed his car keys and the phone. "I'll call you. Stay safe." He opened the door and spoke in hushed tones with Len before turning back to her. Brett waved and raced toward his vehicle.

Keeley watched his Jeep drive down the long driveway, out of her reach. *Lord, comfort him and protect him. Most of all, bring him to You.*

Len cleared his throat. "You okay?"

"I'll be fine. Come in. I'll make us some tea."

"Actually, if you have leaded coffee, I'll take one instead. I think it's gonna be a long night." He locked the door.

Keeley moved into the kitchen and loaded the coffee machine. "Did you get anything else from Davey? Did he reveal who the woman is in their organization?" Thoughts of Beth, Tina and Audrey entered her mind.

"No. Says he's not snitching on his kin." Len plunked down at the table, facing the door. "We're searching for records to determine the home he'd been placed in."

Keeley took some mugs from the cupboard. "Hopefully, you find out soon. I'm tired of running."

"Understood. We're close to—"

Thudding footsteps coming up the stairs silenced his words. Len shot upright, unleashing his weapon.

Pounding sounded on the door. "Keeley, it's Mom. Let me in."

"What's she doing here?" Len holstered his gun, then unlocked and opened the door. "Judge, you're supposed to be staying put. Where's Terry?"

"I ditched him." She stepped inside. "I got Keeley's text to get here right away."

Keeley dropped her mug on the counter. "Text? What text?"

Her mother strode into the kitchen and held out her phone. "This one."

Keeley inched closer.

Mom, need you at the cabin right away. Here are the directions. Come quickly. Alone. My safety depends on it.

Keeley's jaw dropped. "Mom, I didn't send you a text."

Her mother staggered backward. "Then who did?"

Once again, Len unholstered his weapon. "Brett told me you have access to guns. Get one. I'm going to call it in and secure the perimeter. Lock the door and don't let anyone else in." He raised his gun and opened the door, rushing outside.

"Mom, stay low and get on the couch." Keeley bolted the

door, hurried to the cabinet, punched in the code and withdrew the Glock.

"Keeley, who's doing this to our family?" Her mother's hushed words revealed her alarm.

"I wish I knew." Keeley straightened. "Wait. If they were able to hack into your phone, make it look like I texted you, then they could do the same to Brett."

"Where is he?"

"He got a text telling him to come to his father's house because he was dying." Tears welled. "I have to call him before—"

The door crashed open, splintering the wood.

Keeley pivoted, raising her weapon.

And stared down the end of a double-barreled shotgun. Terror coursed through her body, icing her veins.

"You're not going anywhere," the mocking voice said. "Drop it, Keeley, or your mama dies." The woman shifted her aim to Olivia Ash.

The Glock slipped from Keeley's hands when she realized the mama of the Diglo brothers had been under her nose the entire time.

Keeley stumbled forward. "You."

SEVENTEEN

Silence greeted Brett as he entered his father's foyer. Hospital smells wafted in the area, and he suppressed the sadness overtaking his emotions. *Put on a brave face, Brett. For Dad.*

Brett dashed toward his father's room and eased open the door. Stillness permeated the area.

Nancy was nowhere to be seen.

Odd. Wouldn't she stay close to his dad's side in his hour of need?

He moved to the chair beside his father's bed, taking his hand. "I'm here, Dad."

His frail cop father fluttered his eyes open. "Hey, son."

Tears welled at his father's whispered greeting. Brett swallowed the lump forming in his throat. *Keep it together.* "How are you feeling?"

His father turned his head, and a tiny smile formed on his face. "Better now that you're here. How's my grandson?"

"As spunky as ever. I heard him say he wants me to marry Keeley so we can all live together."

"Well, are you?" Brett's father squeezed his hand. "I would be ecstatic to know you've found love before I leave this world."

"Dad, Keeley hasn't forgiven me for leaving. At least, that's what I sense. She keeps pulling back."

"Do you admit MJ is your son?"

"I do. Even without a DNA test." Brett checked his father's pulse. Fairly strong.

Odd.

Wouldn't it be weaker in his last hours?

"That's good, son. Then what are you waiting for? Tell her how you feel."

Brett stood and placed his hand on his dad's forehead. No temp. "How can I when I don't know myself?"

"It's written all over your face. You've fallen for her and your son. Time to form a family."

Was that true?

His father coughed.

Brett lifted the glass on the nightstand and tipped the straw to the man's lips. "Drink."

His father obeyed. "Son, sit. We need to talk."

Brett plunked back in the chair. "About what?"

"Have you thought any more about what I said to you regarding promising to come back to God?"

Brett huffed and slumped back. "Dad, don't—"

"Listen to me carefully. God uses our tough circumstances to shape and grow us." He retook Brett's hand. "But the question remains—will you let Him? It's time. You've been holding on to the past for too long." His father squeezed tightly.

While the question gnawed at Brett, his father's strong hold perplexed him.

Nancy shuffled into the room, carrying clean towels. "Oh, hey, Brett. What are you doing here?"

Brett froze. "Didn't you text me to come?"

"I did no such thing." She placed the towels on a shelf by the window. "Why would you think that?"

Brett flew to his feet. "You said Dad only had a short time left and to get home."

"Son, I'm stronger than I was last week. God is giving me more time to spend with you, Keeley and my sweet grandson."

If Nancy hadn't texted him, then who had?

Images of crossbones on Keeley's laptop flashed through his mind.

No! The Diglo brothers had gotten to them.

He kissed his dad's forehead. "Dad, pray. Keeley and MJ are in danger. I need to go. Love you."

"You too."

Brett brought out the sat phone and dialed the other sat's number. He ran through the house and out to his Jeep as he waited.

And waited.

No answer.

He dialed Antoine. "Pick up. Pick up."

"Constable Antoine."

"Len! What's going on? Where's Keeley?" Brett started the engine.

"She's with her mother in the cabin."

"Olivia is there?" Brett backed out of the driveway and onto the street, squealing his tires. "How did she know where we were?"

"Not sure. Listen, I've secured the perimeter and I'm on my way back to them. We just got a hit on who the foster brothers were adopted by."

"Who?"

"The names are Donald and—"

A commotion cut off his words.

"Len! What's going on?"

For the third time tonight, silence greeted Brett. And he hated silence. He accelerated and turned onto the highway back toward the cabin.

Lord, protect my family.

Keeley's pulse hammered as she fought to keep her breathing under control. *You can't hyperventilate. Not now.* She breathed in, exhaling in extended breaths. She clung to her weeping mother, who crumpled at the sight of the head of the Diglo brothers.

Audrey Todd.

"How could you, Audrey?" It all came into plain view for Keeley. The woman knew plants and would know how poisons worked. Plus, Keeley now remembered why Eddie had seemed so familiar when she'd seen his face at the hunter's cabin. A picture of him had fallen out of Audrey's bag, and she'd scooped it up quickly, but Keeley had caught a glimpse of it.

Stupid, Keeley. You should have remembered that before. Now it's too late.

Audrey's sneer transformed into an evil expression. The normally kind woman vanished.

Had it all been an act?

Audrey raised the shotgun higher. "Yous should have left well enough alone. My Eddie is gone, and now Davey is with the coppers."

Keeley noted her switch of dialect. She obviously put on a front while at college but now returned to her backcountry way of speech. Like her sons.

"You killed my sister and kidnapped my son." Fire burned in Keeley's gut. "How could a mother do that?"

"Easy. Them hikers should have stayed buried. You were too close to pinning their deaths on my boys. I had to get you to back off. Tried to steal your evidence, but you were too smart." She advanced farther into the cabin. "I gave yous your boy back, but what did you do? You kept digging."

"That case had to be solved. Anyone with a conscience would realize that. How did you find us here?"

Audrey pointed to Keeley's purse on a nearby chair. "Easy. I put Bluetooth tags in your purse when you weren't looking. We've just been waiting for the perfect opportunity to strike. Now's that time."

A wave of angst threatened to immobilize Keeley. *Keep it together.* She squeezed her mother tighter. "Why did you lure my mother here? She has nothing to do with this."

"I had to. I couldn't let a judge go free after I kill her daughter." She snickered. "But don't worry. We's not gonna kill MJ. Me and my kin are gonna raise him in the backcountry."

"You will not have my son!" Keeley pulled her mother to a standing position.

"You took mine. I'm taking yours." She turned her head. "Ivan! Get in here."

A burly man dressed in a hunter's jacket sauntered through the entrance. "Yes, Mama?"

"Find the kid." Audrey pointed to the bedrooms.

Ivan moved toward the closed doors.

"No! Don't you touch my grandson." Keeley's mother flew at Ivan.

Audrey fired, hitting Olivia in the shoulder. She dropped.

"Mom!" Keeley rushed to her side and squatted, wrapping her arms around her mother. "Stay with me." She snatched a blanket from the couch and pressed it on her mother's wound.

Audrey scoffed. "She's okay. For now."

Keeley must save her family. *Think, Keels. Think.* Where were the constables? She prayed Len had contacted his fellow officers. She needed to give them time to get here. "Tell me, are your sons foster kids?"

She chuckled. "I guess you can tell they don't look like their mama, huh? All my boys were gifts from God to Donald and I. We took 'em in and raised 'em to live off God's creations. Taught 'em to shoot, archery, axe throwin'. You name it, Donald taught them."

Her mother moaned.

"Which one of them is your hacker?" Keeley pressed harder on her mother's wound.

"*Pfft.* That was me. Them boys barely know how to operate a cell phone."

"Where did you learn to do all that?"

Audrey took one hand off the shotgun and blew on her nails, wiping them on her shirt. "Taught myself. Well, had some help from my video-gaming buddies."

"I'm impressed. Not everyone can hack into someone's computer." Keeley would play up the woman's strength. Try to get on her good side. "Did you also form this fugitive-hiding business?"

Ivan walked to the next room after he'd searched Brett's room.

Nausea attacked Keeley. *Lord, protect my boy!*

"Sure did. I put word out on the dark web that if anyone was lookin' for refuge and a way to flee the country, they just had to pay me. I's had the means to give 'em a new identity." She tapped her temple. "Told ya. Smart mama. You see, I had to provide for my sons, and my teaching career wasn't cutting it, especially since my beloved passed two years ago and left us with nothin'." She placed her hand on her heart. "God rest his soul."

Footsteps thudded on the cabin's front steps, and another man entered. "Mama, we's ready. Bombs is set."

Bombs? Plural?

Keeley's jaw dropped. "What are you talking about?"

Audrey gestured toward the man. "This here's the brainchild, Roy. Say hi, Roy."

He waved. "Mama, can I go get him now?"

Get who?

Audrey patted the top of Roy's head. "Good boy. Yes, go claim your reward."

The bearded Roy with the messy hair knelt in front of Keeley and caressed her face.

Keeley shuddered. "Stay away from me."

"Eddie was right about you. Yous are purdy." He lifted a wad of her hair and sniffed, dragging her closer before planting a rough kiss on her lips.

She fought the urge to cry, but squared her shoulders. She would not give this man the satisfaction.

Roy pushed himself back to his feet. "Now I'm going to kill your boyfriend. It was Mama who texted him. We had to separate you. By now, he's probably figured it out and is on his way back. At least, that's what I'm counting on." He withdrew a nine millimeter. "I'm gonna be waiting in the trees." He charged out of the cabin.

"No! Leave Brett alone. Take me."

Audrey guffawed. "Don't bother. He's out for revenge. You all will pay. And to answer your question, we know where all the evidence is, including the boots you took from Eddie. We're bombing everything. Your lab. Coroner's lab. I also sent a virus to your systems since I failed to destroy it the first time. And if anyone dies?" She shrugged. "So be it."

"But why now? Why didn't you do that days ago?"

She removed a rag from her back pocket and rubbed her shotgun. "Isn't this guy a beaut? I like to make it shine. Gave it to Donald on his last birthday." Her voice quivered. She cleared her throat. "Anyway, been kind of busy with them fugitives. You know the sayin'—'If you're gonna do something, do it right.' I needed time to get ready." She stuffed the rag away and raised the weapon. "Now's the time."

"You're sick. I can't believe you fooled me all this time."

Ivan returned, holding a sleeping MJ. "Mama, this little guy is a sound sleeper. Didn't hear me. I like him."

Keeley blasted to her feet. "Give me my son!"

Audrey backhanded Keeley across the face.

She stumbled backward, her hand flying to her cheek to soothe the sting.

Come on, Len. Where are you?

Keep her talking. "Where did you get the privet to poison me?"

"Where do you think? Imported it, then planted it on my property."

"And where is that?"

Ivan carried MJ from the cabin.

"Not far from here. We hid it well." She aimed the shotgun

in her direction. "Hand over your cell phone. We can't have them tracking you now, can we?"

Keeley hauled her sleeve farther down her wrist to hide her smartwatch, then extracted her phone from her back pocket and held it out.

Audrey threw it on the couch. "Now, get your mother. We're leaving. You don't want to be here to see my Roy kill your love."

Keeley stuffed the laces of her hiking boots inside and fumbled to put them on as a thought shot through her mind.

They were out of time.

And no help had arrived to save them.

Brett parked on the side of the cabin's driveway to hide his approach. He had to enter by stealth mode. He wouldn't risk giving away his presence…for Keeley and MJ's sake. Brett had gotten in touch with Constable Jackson and requested assistance, but Jackson informed him they were responding to a suspected bomb threat in Carimoose Bay. However, he'd leave another officer in charge and be there as soon as he could. *Hurry!*

Fishing out the flashlight from his glove box to use as a weapon, Brett silently chastised himself for not bringing his rifle along. He had to get to his father's gun collection. He stepped out of his Jeep and inched toward the cabin, moving from tree to tree to keep himself concealed. *Lord, I know I haven't trusted You, but I need Your guidance and help in saving my family. I love them and can't lose them now…just when I found them.*

He peeked out from the tree in front of his father's cabin, searching for any movement. Their daylight was diminishing quickly, and soon darkness would be upon them.

Stillness blanketed the area, including the cabin. *Lord, help them to just be hiding.* However, his gut was telling him something was wrong.

Terribly wrong.

Once Brett ensured he was alone, he dashed to the veranda and bounded up the steps. It was then he noticed the demolished door. *No!* "Keels! Where are you?" His hushed cry amplified in the small area.

Silence greeted him.

Again.

Creak.

He pivoted.

A bearded hunter stood on the step with his gun aimed at Brett's heart. "Welcome home. I's been waiting for your return. I'm Roy, and you're about to die for killing my baby brother."

Brett's heartbeat jackhammered, sending terror to every part of his body.

Give me strength, Lord.

"Where is my family?" He took a step toward the hunter. "If you've done anything to hurt them, I'll—"

Roy lifted his nine millimeter higher. "You'll what?"

Brett gripped the flashlight tighter, contemplating a takedown scenario. He observed the open gun cabinet. Could he outrun a bullet?

Hardly.

"You'll never make it. If you want to see them, drop the flashlight." Roy shot up the rest of the steps. "Now!"

Brett didn't have a choice. He let his only weapon slip from his fingers.

Roy grabbed Brett by the arm and pushed him off the veranda. "Get moving."

"Where are we going?"

"To sleep." Roy hit him on the head.

Brett's legs buckled, and he felt himself falling. A thought arose as the darkness called out to him.

The man hadn't worn a mask.

That only meant one thing.

They wouldn't leave anyone alive.

EIGHTEEN

"Get out of the vehicle!"

Keeley shuddered at Audrey's sharp command. "Where's my son?"

"Don't worry—he's right behind us. You'll see him soon. Now get out."

Keeley opened the truck door and exited the vehicle before helping her mother.

Her mother winced at the movement.

Lord, she's losing blood. Please send help. "Mom, press on your wound."

"I'm so tired." Judge Ash's weakened voice conveyed her condition.

"I've got you." Keeley wrapped her arm around her mother's waist and surveyed her surroundings. But only trees were in her path. "Where are we?"

Audrey raised her shotgun. "See that cluster of trees? Go."

Keeley and her mother hobbled through the opening until they came to a clearing. Keeley stopped short.

They had multiple small structures built into different rock formations. Camouflaged trees hung over each building. Some cliffs were in the distance.

No wonder they'd stayed hidden from the world.

She spun around to face Audrey. "You live underground?"

"Best place to be." She waved her gun toward a patch of low-lying bushes. "That way."

Keeley examined the area Audrey had referred to and almost missed it. Vegetation hid a latch. "What's in there?"

"Our tornado shelter, or as I like to put it, your grave. Open it."

Goose bumps slithered up Keeley's neck, and she forced herself to move. She reached between the plants and pulled on the handle. The lid opened, and she pushed it forward, exposing steep rock steps leading into a black hole.

There was no way her mother could make it down them. "My mom is too feeble."

A vehicle sounded, and then a door slammed.

Audrey tipped her head and sneered. "Well then, help her. You don't have a choice, or I will shoot your son, who just arrived. Go or watch him die."

"No. Don't hurt him." Keeley gently nudged her mother's arm. "Mom, I'll go first and help you take one step at a time. Okay?"

She nodded.

It took them a few minutes to reach the bottom, guided only by a small beam of light coming from somewhere deep in the ground.

Keeley clung to her mother and moved forward. "Where to, Audrey?"

The woman yanked on a string, flooding the shelter with bright light.

Keeley blinked to allow time for her eyes to adjust. A small room stocked with shelves containing jars of food, flashlights, batteries and other preservation supplies came into view.

"Welcome to your dungeon. Don't worry, *Keels*. You won't be here long." Audrey gestured toward her mother. "But she will die here."

Keeley gasped. "Don't do this. We won't tell anyone. I'll help you destroy the evidence." Could she really uphold that promise?

"Sit." Audrey pointed to the round table and chairs next to the shelves.

Keeley helped her mother into one of the chairs.

"Mama!" Her son's scream sent shivers throughout Keeley's body.

"MJ!"

Ivan appeared around the corner, holding MJ. He squirmed in the man's arms, kicking and screaming. Ivan charged forward and practically threw MJ into Keeley's arms. "You take the brat." He turned to his mother. "Mama, I'm not so sure we's should keep him. He's feisty."

Keeley hugged a crying MJ tightly and dropped into the chair. "Shhh, it's okay, slugger. I've got you, and God's got us."

Audrey slapped the back of Ivan's head. "Simmer down and get ahold of yourself. We need to go prepare."

Prepare for what?

Audrey marched into Keeley's personal space and poked her in the arm. "You keep MJ quiet. We'll be back."

"Where are you going?"

"None of your business, and don't try screaming. There's no one around these parts. Just my kin and I. Oh…and a few wanted fugitives. They ain't gonna help ya." She addressed Ivan. "Let's go."

They headed up the steps, and seconds later, the latch door slammed shut, followed by a dead bolt.

They were locked in with nowhere to run.

Brett stirred. His head pounded. He forced his eyes open and stared into pitch blackness. He touched the bump where Roy had smashed his gun into and winced. Panic pummeled him. He had to escape, but where was he? How long had he been out?

Brett ignored the questions and placed his hands on the damp, broken floor. Cement. He pushed himself into a seated position and rubbed his eyes to clear his vision. It didn't help. The darkness blanketed him, sending another wave of panic surging throughout his body. A steady drip of water sounded nearby. Musk assaulted his nose.

Great. Roy took him to a similar place Brett had never wanted to be again.

Somewhere underground. Brett flashed back to being a five-year-old boy when he'd gotten locked in his grandparents' root cellar for hours. It was where his fear of confinement began.

God uses our tough circumstances to shape and grow us. Will you let Him?

His father's words once again filtered through Brett's brain. It was time to allow God to change him.

Brett drew his knees to his chest and rested his head. *God is the only one who can help me now. God, I should have come to You years ago. How could I have been so blind? You've been right beside me, haven't You?*

Brett sighed. *You've taken me into the wilderness to make me a better man, and I've failed You. I'm sorry. Please forgive me. Create in me a clean heart. A new heart.*

I surrender whatever is left of my life to You.

Show me how to save Keels and my son. I love them.

Tears flowed freely, cleansing Brett of his past. His failures. His guilt over Gideon's death. His anger at losing his mother. Of his father's sickness.

Everything.

Peace washed over him in only one way he knew was possible.

Through God.

Adrenaline powered his body, sending strength into his muscles and a thought racing into his mind. *Find a way out.*

He stood and felt his way around the damp walls, his feet crunching on pieces of broken cement floor. Finally, he reached a wooden door. He glided his hands over the exit, looking for any flaws. His fingers stopped at the top hinge. The pin was exposed from the barrel. If he forced it out, along with the others, he'd be able to escape. But what could he use?

The darkness prevented him from seeing anything.

Brett dropped to his knees and ran his hands along the cement floor, crawling around the room as he prayed.

He struck a hard object.

A chunk of broken concrete.

Lord, help it to work.

He gripped the tool and fumbled his way back to the door. *Help them not to hear me.* Brett held his breath and placed the cement under the pin's lip, thrusting upward again and again until it loosened enough for Brett to pry it out.

He did the same to the others, then heaved the door open from the hinge side.

A dim light greeted him, and he blinked, allowing his eyes to adjust before moving forward.

He examined his surroundings and spotted cement steps going upward. Brett inched along the wall, concealing his approach and listening for his attackers. He stopped at the bottom of the stairs and peeked around the corner.

Empty.

He took one step at a time to silence his hiking boots. When he reached the top, he tried the doorknob. Unlocked.

He guessed they figured he was in a locked room and that would keep him contained. However—

God provided a way.

Brett eased the door open and slipped outside.

Darkness had descended.

He let his eyes focus, then looked around and surveyed his surroundings.

Brett was deep in the forest.

But where?

He glanced upward. Even the clouds hid the moon, blocking its light.

And any hope of guiding him through a maze of trees to find his family.

* * *

Keeley rocked MJ until he stilled. She had to stay quiet to keep him calm. She rested her chin on the top of his head. *Lord, show us a way out of this mess. Save us. Save Brett.* She observed her mother. Her ashen face told Keeley her mother's weakened state would make it impossible for the group to act quickly if the need arose. "Mom, you okay?"

"Tired. And ashamed."

"Why?"

"I've been a fool, Keeley." She reached out and grabbed Keeley's hand. "I've failed you and have been a terrible mother. I see that now. I'm just sorry it took tragedy to open my eyes."

How could Keeley stay mad at her mother at a time like this? After all, God forgave Keeley for all her mistakes. It was time for Keeley to do the same.

"Mom—"

"Let me finish. I should have told you about Zoe. I should have kept Zoe. My pride and desire for fame blinded me into not doing what God wanted me to." She squeezed Keeley's hand harder. "That's why I tried so hard to make it up to Zoe. I shut you out and gave her my love. I robbed you of a sister's love. For that, I wouldn't blame you if you never forgive me."

Keeley let her mother's apology sink in.

"Honey, I'm so sorry. Sorry for a lot of things." Her mother bit her lip. "Most of all, I'm sorry for not telling you how proud I am of you. Of the woman and mother you've become. Of the work you do. I love you and MJ to the moon and back." She inhaled. "I just wish I'd have told you sooner and not at such a precarious time as this."

A tear slipped down Keeley's cheek.

These were words she had longed to hear for years.

Keeley leaned forward and wrapped her free arm around her mother. "I forgive you, Mom, and I love you, too."

Tears flowed from the eyes of a powerful Supreme Court judge.

Her mother.

"I'm proud of you, too, Mom."

Clapping erupted from behind them. "Aw, ain't that sweet. Making up for lost time?"

They both startled.

Audrey removed a nine millimeter from her waistline. "I'm afraid your time is up. Keeley, you're coming with me. Stand."

Keeley hesitated. *Lord, help!*

MJ jolted awake and screamed.

Audrey thrust the gun's barrel into her mother's temple. "Give MJ to your mother or I'll blow 'er brains out right in front of your son."

"Okay, okay." Keeley kissed her son's forehead and stood. "Mama's gotta go, MJ, but you'll be okay here with Gramma."

"No, Mama!"

Keeley forced her tears back and handed her son to her mother. "It will be okay. I promise."

Audrey wrenched Keeley's arm and leaned in. "Don't make promises you can't keep. Now go! And, Judge Ash, don't try anything. Ivan is guarding the entrance. You won't escape him. His papa taught him well."

Keeley blew her son and mother kisses. "Love you guys."

More tears from both of them tore at Keeley's heart as she forced her legs to move up the rock steps and into the darkness.

Rain pelted the region. Keeley lifted her face and let the drops soothe her skin. Peace washed over her.

She knew its source.

Her Father. Her life was in His hands.

"Ivan, kill them if they try to escape. I'll be back." Audrey pushed Keeley. "March."

She stumbled but caught her footing. "Where are we going?"

"Straight ahead." Audrey flicked on a flashlight, powering a beam toward the cliffs in the distance.

Horror gripped Keeley by the throat, smothering her air. The woman was leading her to her death. "You don't have to do this."

"Yes, I do." She poked Keeley in the back with her gun.

Keeley walked, listening to her son's screams lessen as she moved farther from the shelter. She stopped at the edge and turned to face her accuser, a plan forming in her mind. Her only ray of hope. Something she'd learned in a self-defense class.

"You won't get away with this. You—" Keeley doubled over, pretending to be in pain.

"What's wrong with—"

Keeley thrust her body forward, bulldozing herself into Audrey.

They both fell to the ground as Audrey's gun fired into the air.

Keeley yanked on the woman's hair.

"You brat!" Audrey clawed Keeley's face.

Keeley rolled away and scrambled to her feet as one hiking boot slipped off.

Audrey bolted upright and lunged.

Keeley sidestepped out of her path, but not far enough.

Audrey clutched Keeley's ankle as she plummeted over the cliff's edge, taking Keeley with her.

Their combined screams pierced the night. Audrey let go of Keeley and plunged down the rocky incline.

Free of Audrey's grip, Keeley fumbled to grab anything to break her fall. *Lord, help!*

Her wrist slammed against the rocks, and dirt peppered her face moments before she felt a tree root. She latched on to the lifeline tightly and dug the toe of her left boot into the cliff's edge, slowing her descent.

Her feet landed on a narrow ledge, breaking her fall. She clung to the root and cowered against the cliff's side.

The rain had ended but had soaked her clothing.

She shivered and tapped her smartwatch to send out an SOS to emergency services.

And prayed.

* * *

Brett sprinted toward the gunshot that had echoed through the forest a few minutes ago. *Lord, help Keels and MJ to be okay.* Thankfully, the rain had subsided. For now. He stumbled through a wooded area and stopped at the sound of a loud male voice. He hid behind a large tree.

"Roy, what do you mean, kill the kid?" the voice asked. "I know he's a brat, but I thought Mama wanted to keep him."

Brett drew in an uneven breath. MJ! *Lord, no! Show me where my son is.* He poked his head out but kept himself concealed.

A slim, bearded man stood beside a cluster of low-lying bushes, waving a flashlight beam in different directions. "Fine. I'll do it. Where's Mama? I's heard a shot earlier." A pause. "Me neither. She took that redhead to get rid of her."

What? No! Brett blinked back the tears forming. Had he found the love of his life only to lose her?

"Yup, the mother and kid are still here in the bunker." He swore. "Stop telling me what to do, Roy. Yous better get here to help me bury the bodies." He clicked off the call, leaned down and opened a door hidden among the bushes. He unleashed a gun and disappeared into an underground hole.

Brett's pulse skipped a beat. He had to save his son and Olivia. *Lord, give me strength to overpower this brother.* He zipped toward the opening and searched for any type of weapon. He spied a large branch and scooped it up, praying as he descended the rock steps. Thankfully, a dim light coming from below lit his way.

"Leave him alone!" Olivia yelled in the distance.

Brett inched along the corridor, staying as quiet as he could with both hands tightly wound around the stick.

MJ whimpered.

Brett stole a peek.

The brother stood with his back to Brett, pointing a gun at MJ. He had to act now or lose his son.

Brett tiptoed closer. He raised his makeshift weapon, mustered strength and thrust the branch down hard on the man's head.

The brother dropped.

"Brett!" Olivia pushed herself upright. "Thank the Lord."

Brett dropped the stick and lifted MJ. "You okay, sport?"

The boy responded by burying his head in Brett's chest.

Olivia wrapped her arms around Brett. "Thank you. Find Keeley. Audrey took her."

"Audrey Todd? She's Mama?"

"Yes." Olivia rubbed her shoulder and winced.

The hunter stirred.

Brett set MJ down, then scooped up the man's sat phone and gun. "Hurry, let's get out of here and lock him in. Can you walk?"

She nodded. "The bleeding has lessened. I'll be okay. God will give me strength."

The trio trudged up the stairs, and Brett slammed the door shut, locking the Diglo brother inside.

"Not so fast, Mr. Paramedic," a menacing voice said behind them.

Brett spun around and raised the gun, moving in front of his family.

"You're smarter than I thought you was." Roy had a shotgun aimed at the trio. "Give it up. There's no escapin' my kin and me."

"Leave us alone. I used to be a cop and have impeccable aim." Brett widened his stance in protective mode.

"Well then, we's got us a good ole-fashioned shoot-out here." Roy snickered. "Who will win? The hunter or the ex-copper-turned-paramedic? Yous still a good shot?"

"I killed your brother, didn't I?" Brett hated to antagonize him, but perhaps the man's anger would catch him off guard.

"Why, you…" Roy lifted his gun higher and charged toward him.

Brett fired, hitting Roy in the shoulder.

Shouts sounded in the woods.

Lights bouncing through the trees lit up the forest like fireflies on the East Coast.

Jackson and multiple constables charged through the tree line, weapons raised. "Police! Stand down."

Brett placed his weapon on the ground. "Layke, Roy is armed, but I shot him in the shoulder."

Jackson rushed forward and scooped the shotgun up, pointing his gun at the moaning brother. "Move again and you'll be sorry." He turned to another constable. "Get him in cuffs and take him away."

"Is Antoine okay?" Brett wiped his forehead with the back of his hand.

"Yes. We found him passed out in the trees by your cabin. Paramedics are on their way here."

"How did you find us?"

Jackson raised a device. "Keeley's SOS from her smartwatch." He pointed behind Brett. "In that direction."

Fear coursed through Brett's body, depleting his energy. *Stay strong. For Keels and your son.* "Olivia, can you and MJ stay with the constables?"

She nodded.

Brett addressed Jackson. "I'm coming with you, Layke. Let's go."

The duo dashed through the trees and to the cliff's edge.

Jackson pointed. "The reading is coming from down there."

Brett followed the direction where Jackson had indicated.

A single hiking boot sat on its side at the cliff's edge.

"No!" Brett grabbed Jackson's light and shone it over the side.

Keeley sat cowered on a narrow ledge.

She was alive.

Thank You, Lord. "Keels!"

"Brett." She lifted her face in their direction, her eyes widening in the light's beam. "You're alive!"

Jackson spoke into his radio, requesting Search and Rescue. "What do you mean? That's too long, and another storm is predicted to hit soon. We need them now." A pause. "Fine." He hung up and turned to Brett. "They're on their way but can't be here for six hours."

"But we have to get to her. Now!" Brett hated his forceful words, but he had to rescue the woman he loved.

Jackson squeezed Brett's shoulder. "We will." He glanced over the side. "Good—she's not too far down. The ledge saved her life."

Once again, Brett peered over, shining the light on the cliff's wall. Roots and tree branches poked out. They must have stopped her descent. "Keels, are you okay?"

"Head hurts. Soaked. Freezing. Help." Her broken words revealed a weakened condition.

"Help is on the way. We'll get to you as quick as we can!" Jackson shouted back. "Hold tight."

"Where's Audrey?" Brett asked.

Keeley pointed downward.

The mama of the Diglo brothers had fallen to her death.

Brett tugged Jackson away from the edge. "Listen, do you have spotlights and climbing gear of any kind in your cruiser?"

"Yes. What are you thinking?"

"I've been training with SAR, as they want a paramedic on their team. I can get to her."

"It's too dangerous, and you're still in training. We have to wait for daylight and the team."

Brett pointed to the edge. "Would you wait if it was Hannah down there?"

Even in the darkness, Brett didn't miss the constable's softened eyes. "No. You love her, don't you?"

"I do. I can do this. Get the gear here now."

"It's risky, Brett."

Brett let out a hissed sigh. "I know, but it's *my* risk."

Jackson hit his radio button and spoke to his team, requesting any spotlights and gear they had in their cruisers. "Okay, now we wait."

"Thank you." Brett returned to the edge. "Keels, I'm coming to get you."

Two hours later, Brett guided Keeley out of Olivia's hospital room to a lounge across the hall. Brett had rappelled down the side of the cliff and gotten her to safety with the help of spotlights, a harness and an axe they'd found on the Diglos' property. Paramedics had checked her for injuries before she reunited with Olivia and MJ. Right now, MJ slept, cuddled on a chair by his gramma's hospital bed—safe and sound. Doctors had examined Keeley and confirmed she just had bumps and bruises. No concussion.

Police had arrested the other brother, so all Diglos were in custody. SAR would look for Audrey's body at daybreak.

"Keels, I need to tell you something." Brett gestured to vacant seats in the room's corner.

They sat.

He took her hands in his. "I'm so glad you're okay. I thought I lost you. Again." His voice shook, exposing his emotions.

"What are you saying, Brett?"

"I need to tell you why I wouldn't believe you about MJ." He inhaled deeply, gathering his thoughts. "I once had a woman lie to me, claiming I had fathered her child when I knew I hadn't. It was after I changed my wayward life."

Keeley's eyes widened. "That's why you wouldn't believe me? I get it, but that's not me. I wouldn't lie to you about something like that or anything."

"I realize that now, and I know MJ is mine." He chuckled. "I don't need a DNA test, as he's exactly like me."

Keeley smiled. "Right?"

"I also wanted to tell you that I've surrendered my heart to God. I've been a fool for doubting Him."

"I'm so glad."

Brett hesitated in asking the question he dreaded. She had distanced herself from him over the past few days. Did she want him in her life?

"What is it, Brett?" She rubbed his hand with her thumb.

Their gazes locked, and he tucked a wiry curl behind her ear. "I'm not going anywhere, and I want you back in my life. But my question is, do you want me in yours?"

She looked away.

Brett held his breath.

Keeley turned back to him, a smile dancing on her lips. "I've waited so long to hear you say that. It's my turn to tell you something. Besides being scared you were leaving, I've had a hard time opening up to you because another man, Preston, made promises to both me and MJ, but he left and broke our hearts."

Brett leaned in. "Keels, I'm not Preston. I'm not going anywhere." He leaned closer, staring into her eyes. "I love you."

She let out a soft cry. "Me too."

He placed his hand behind her head, pulling her toward him. Their lips met in a tender kiss.

Brett released her. "I can't wait to tell MJ I'm his father and we're going to be a family."

The pitter-patter of feet filled the room.

They turned.

MJ ran toward them. "You're my papa? For reals?"

Brett stood and lifted him, twirling MJ. "I am, son."

"Yippee!"

Brett chuckled and stopped twirling, bringing Keeley closer. "We're a family."

Words from his father reentered Brett's mind.

God brings His people into the wilderness to shape them.

Brett now believed the truth in those words. Not only had God shaped him, but He eliminated his doubts and welcomed Brett back into His family.

And it was the only place Brett wanted to be.

EPILOGUE

Seven months later

Keeley hummed the carol playing on the stereo and placed the last ornament on the Christmas tree at Harold Ryerson's cabin. She inspected her work and smiled before glancing out the window. Snow floated like feathers, bringing holiday cheer one week before the official date when Christians rejoiced in Jesus's birth. MJ insisted they spend Christmas Day at the cabin, and Brett agreed. Much had happened in the past seven months, and they had lots to celebrate.

SAR had found Audrey's body the morning after the attack. Keeley struggled with the woman's death, even though she'd been the source of all their troubles. Keeley counted her older colleague as a friend. Beth had apologized to her for her abruptness but confessed how her worry for their safety got the better of her. The Diglos were devastated at their mother's death and tried to blame everything on Keeley. They still denied their involvement in any criminal activity and killing the mayor's daughter—Keeley's half sister. However, after studying the vegetation around the Diglos' hidden underground structures, Keeley linked seeds on their boots and clothing to the poisonous privet growing in a concealed greenhouse on their property. They'd imported the seeds, which was their downfall. The plant couldn't be found anywhere else in the

Yukon. Plus, Davey, the younger of the brothers left, finally tattled on the others, explaining how Eddie Bishop—the brother Brett had killed—had stumbled upon Zoe and her boyfriend too close to their hidden property. They had agreed the couple had to die, rather than taking the risk of them exposing their organization to the police. The hikers had simply been in the wrong place at the wrong time.

Police also found three wanted criminals hidden on the Diglos' property. The fugitives had revealed everything they knew about the underground organization, clinching the evidence stacked against them.

Keeley's mother had healed from her shotgun wound and welcomed Brett into the family with open arms.

Doctors had also surprised them all by stating Brett's father had gone into remission, so the group indeed had lots to be thankful for.

Brett and Layke had quickly become best friends after the ordeal. Layke had called to tell them Hannah had a baby girl, and they'd named her Hope because they were thankful God blessed them against all odds. Kind of like Sarah and Abraham.

Keeley studied the cabin. After they'd shared the news with MJ that Brett was his father, MJ had requested they spend lots of time here. Brett and Harold, along with Keeley's mother, had planned an expansion. They added more bedrooms and a sunroom to the back of the building.

Enough room for everyone.

"You forgot an ornament."

Keeley jumped. "Brett, you scared me." She pointed to the empty box. "No, I didn't. They're all on the tree."

"Are you sure?" Brett snickered.

MJ stepped out from behind his father, holding a plastic marshmallow snowman sitting on a slab of chocolate and graham cracker. "Look close, Mama. There's a surprise for you."

Brett tousled his son's hair. "Sport, you weren't supposed to say anything."

Keeley inched closer for a better look. She gasped and covered her mouth.

An engagement ring hung from the snowman's stick arm.

"I love you with all my heart." Brett knelt, removed the diamond ring and held it out. "Keels, will you marry me?"

She dropped to her knees and flung her arms around him. "Yes! I love you, too."

"Gramma and Grampa, she said yes!"

Keeley pulled out of their embrace as Harold and her mother entered the room.

Her mother clapped. "Praise the Lord!"

"Well, put it on her, son." Harold beamed.

Keeley held out her hand.

Brett slipped the ring on her finger before reaching in and kissing her on the lips.

"Ewww. That's gross." MJ wormed his way in between them.

Laughter filled the cabin as "Joy to the World" played softly in the background.

Yes, indeed. Joy filtered into their world, and Keeley praised God for bringing them through the tough wilderness of life.

He was in every detail, and for that, she was grateful.

* * * * *

Dear Reader,

Thank you for reading Keeley, Brett and MJ's story! I enjoyed diving into the world of forensic botany and researching this field. Anything I embellished for fiction is totally on me. I also loved going back to the fictional town of Carimoose Bay, Yukon, as well as visiting old friends from previous books. It was fun to catch up on their lives. I hope you did as well.

Keeley and Brett struggled with journeying through tough times in the wilderness of life. Knowing God was in every detail of their lives gave them comfort, and they surrendered to Him. They both were able to put their pasts behind them and not only forgive others but themselves. Something we could all learn from, right?

I'd love to hear from you. You can contact me through my website, DarleneLTurner.com, and also sign up for my newsletter to receive exclusive subscriber giveaways. Thanks again for reading my story.

God bless,
Darlene L. Turner